THE LORD'S PINK OCEAN

THE LORD'S PINK OCEAN demonstrates once again David Walker's remarkable versatility. In an isolated valley between steep hills two families survive on either side of a blue lake: the Smiths with their son Ian and the Parkers with their daughter Mary. The lake is one of the few supplies of water supporting life on earth, for pink algae, originally bred by man to scavenge filth, are now lethally out of control in almost every other source.

The Parkers and the Smiths share the freedom of the valley, but they are prisoners of a deadly world outside, prisoners too of one another. With their primitive tools, scanty knowledge and weakened livestock, life for them is that plain struggle for existence which has always been man's fundamental lot. Like people alive on the earth today, these families know fear and desire, hunger and satisfaction, enmity and love, hardship and happiness. But the drone of a flying machine spells danger to them. Inevitably the arrival of visitors and the maturing of Ian and Mary bring mounting conflict and ultimately provide the novel with its powerful climax.

By the same author

DEVIL'S PLUNGE
COME BACK GEORDIE
MALLABEC
WINTER OF MADNESS
STORMS OF OUR JOURNEY
WHERE THE HIGH WINDS BLOW
SANDY WAS A SOLDIER'S BOY
HARRY BLACK
DIGBY
THE PILLAR
GEORDIE
THE STORM AND THE SILENCE

For children

DRAGON HILL
PIRATE ROCK
BIG BEN

DAVID WALKER

THE LORD'S PINK OCEAN

*

COLLINS

TORONTO AND LONDON

1972

William Collins Sons and Co Ltd
Toronto · London · Glasgow · Sydney
Auckland · Johannesburg

First published 1972
David Walker 1972
ISBN 0 00 221478 4
Set in Monotype Bembo
Made and Printed in Great Britain by
William Collins Sons & Co Ltd Glasgow

1

RUTH stirred, asleep; and their child was sleeping across the cabin. James Parker waited outside until the sun became a full circle above the cliff beyond the lake. Then he turned away from that to face the South. 'Thanks Lord for sparing us,' he said. He thanked the Lord each morning, sun or cloud or fog or rain or snow, in fierce winds and cold, in lightning and thunder. But on a morning of kindly weather a man could say his thanks more happily.

The few birds were busy, the chickadees that came to eat his crumbs, the small brown creeper climbing the giant sugar maple. Even that rooster crowed more cockily.

But the sight of that rooster and its hens, of that bull and cattle, of that ram and sheep, took from the happiness of James Parker. They had been fine birds and beasts when James was young, he remembered that well. But now, for all his good grass and grain, they were sorry creatures. He did not know why. There were neither wise men nor books to help him.

He looked across the lake at Robert Smith's untidy farm. Like his own, it lay on sloping land between cliff and water. Unlike his own, the paddock fences were broken down, the firewood heaped anyhow, the barn roof sagging, the vegetable patch yellow with mustard, the grass growing rankly at the cabin. He did not deserve this weakling calf, but Smith deserved that dead sheep on its back.

He milked the cow that was yielding, and all she gave was one pitcher, barely enough for their growing child. Then he took his axe, and was walking towards the calf to knock it on the head when he heard a call from over the water.

It was Robert Smith, pointing his arm to the foot of the lake. They went there each day, but at different hours, the good farmer soon after dawn, the lazy farmer when the sun was high. Robert Smith never wanted to meet James Parker unless he wanted something out of him.

It's only a quarter of a mile across the lake, his mother used to say, *but a long long way, and that is how it should be. They're not our kind of people.* His mother had remembered many things from Times Before, and she had said: *It's your duty to help your neighbour, James.*

The dew was cool underfoot as he crossed the pasture to the trodden path that led along the shore. A trout rose out there, and ripples spread in the clear blue water.

James stopped, and turned with a memory. It had been at this very place when the leaves were bright, his hand in his mother's. *Look!* she said. The great birds circled once, calling, and then glided down to mighty splashings, he could see them still in the eye of his mind. *The poor wild geese*, she said. *Remember them, James.* The geese had stayed until one morning they could no longer break the ice, and they gave strange haunting cries, perhaps of farewell, and flew away to seek warmer places. But the wild geese never came again. No birds ever came to swim in the lake.

It was because of seeing the geese with her when he was so young that James had buried his mother here. He passed her grave and quickened pace to meet his neighbour. It was pleasant to meet another man, even that foxy Robert Smith. The sound of the falls grew louder, not a heavy noise but a splashing far below where the water struck a first ledge and flew out in spray to fall again and splash again.

The two men reached the bridge together, and each opened the livestock gate at his end. *It's a good bridge we made*, Robert

Smith had said when it was finished. That was just like him, because his only work had been his gate. All the rest of the stout log bridge had been built by James Parker.

They were of a size and strength, each wearing only a leather loincloth for the summer weather. 'A fine morning, Neighbour,' James said.

'A grand day for it, Neighbour,' said Robert Smith. Sometimes he would say that as if the grand day for it was a kind of joke. But his face was sombre on this fine morning.

They both turned to look over the lip of the falls, pure water gleaming smoothly to its plunge. They looked past that at the river far below them, flowing on its short course to the sea.

The river was pink, and the ocean was pink as far as man could see. It was the colour of the wild rose that bloomed now by the lake, a colour that glowed with life, as the wild rose glowed alive in the sun. There were threads of pinkness into the backbone of the river, and pink patches of pond and puddle.

But all the land was grey. The ruins of the old town were grey and dead amid that colour and before the sea. 'No change,' said Robert Smith.

'No change,' James Parker said. It was ten summers since the one brief change.

They turned to face one another again across the bridge in their green land at the waterfall.

'How can I serve you?' Parker asked.

Smith smiled in that superior way, but briefly. 'Mebbe we could serve ane anither.' The Smith family spoke in the rough language of people from a Scottish country somewhere. 'First a question – did you folk hear a queer sound in the night?'

James felt a coldness in his neck. This explained why Smith was less rude this morning. 'No,' he said. 'What sound?'

'The woman woke me. *H'sst, Robbie*! she said, but I heard

nothing. It was at the time the moon was setting. *What like a sound*? I asked the woman. But she could not explain it. Not like the wind in the trees, and there was no breath of wind. Not like the rushing of the water. Not like the thunder. More like the rolling of stones and earth . . .'

'We hear that often on the dead hillsides beyond us.'

'Ay, but she said this was a longdrawn sound – growing to a droning buzz, changing in direction, fading. The woman has the sharper ears, and the laddie still sharper, but he was too deep to waken.'

'My woman and the girl have sharper ears, but both sleep soundly. Still, I will ask them. Neighbour,' James said, to give a comfort that he could never quite feel. 'There's no one but us.'

'There's no one but us. It was a fancy of the woman's ears.'

'You said we might serve one another. Was it over this sound?'

'Not that,' Smith said. 'It's in the matter of the livestock. There is a weakness in your livestock that has spread to mine.'

'There is a weakness in your livestock that has spread to mine,' James said, with rightful vexation. Yet the bond of that imagined sound still lingered between them. 'The truth would be that your livestock and mine have both been weakening for a long time now.'

'That's right,' said Smith. He frowned, seeming uneasy, and scratched his broad hairy chest. 'The boy wandered where he shouldn't yesterday,' he said abruptly.

'Not *Outside*?'

'He climbed Outside, but just over the ridge where no water touches except the rain. If I've told him the once, it's been a hundred times, and a good skelping I give him when he came back safe. It's being alone too much that puts him in the mood for mischief. He brought this.'

From the pocket of his breechclout (his kilt, he called it)

Smith drew a round flat metal thing, the size across of a woman's palm, and thrust it at James Parker.

James stared, but he did not dare to touch.

'It's safe, man, what are you feared about? If it wasn't safe, my boy would be dead.'

James took the thing. He could still read most of the words cut into weathered metal. Round the edge of the circle was printed: *Atlantic Livestock Improvement Society*. He read that aloud slowly. Then, to himself, he read the words printed in short rows across the middle of the thing:

> CROSSBRED STEER
> SHORTHORN-ANGUS
> BEST IN SH . . ., 19 . . ., but some letters or

figures of that line were faded from the metal.

> IAN MACDONALD.

'Ian MacDonald,' James Parker said. His own voice sounded strange to him. It was not those names that made his voice sound strange to him.

'The woman's folk bore the name MacDonald, and the woman's Dad was Ian, like we call our boy.' Robert Smith coughed, and turned away to look at the Lord's pink ocean.

'*Crossbred*,' said James Parker. '*Shorthorn-Angus*. But that was a mixing of the blood, surely a sin, so my mother taught me.'

'And mine the same,' said Smith, scratching himself. It would be the fleas, or perhaps the lice, for the Smiths were not decent washers of the body. 'But when the woman saw that thing, she . . .' He hesitated.

Parker handed it back. 'Your woman, you were saying?'

'The woman said that she remembered her mum talk once of such a practice, that it was done in Times Before, giving strength to the beasts. Neighbour, my pure Rhode Islands, my pure Cheviots, my pedigree Angus are become worthless, for all my good care. And yours?'

'My pure Barred Rocks, my pure Merinos, my pedigree Ayrshires are become worthless,' admitted Parker. He shook his head, knowing now the thought that was in Smith's mind. 'It could be sinful,' he said. 'It could bring the wrath of the Lord upon us.'

'I said the same to the woman, but the woman said: *We have already lost the half of our beasts, and soon we will starve, in another winter even. But they are beasts of the field put here by the Lord to feed us and to clothe us. The Lord's law that our mothers taught us is for people, not for the animals.*' Smith chuckled deeply. 'The woman said that she was daft not to remember that old custom. The woman is not daft, but wise for a woman.'

'If there was such a custom of mixing blood between the beasts in Times Before,' James said. 'Mightn't that have been one of their many sins that caused the Lord to strike them?'

'Neighbour, I don't know. But we must take measures, or we shall starve.'

'That is true,' James Parker said. 'I will consult my woman, who is wise for a woman. The Lord go with you, Neighbour.'

'The Lord go with you, Neighbour.'

The great Lord Alga was ever with them, invisible, inscrutable, Lord of tempest and tranquillity.

On his way home James thought about the suggestion made to him by Robert Smith, who was in most ways foolish, just how foolish was shown by the fact that he had not long ago disciplined his son against climbing out of the valley. And yet the boy's discovery – it might be true that the mixing of blood between the common beasts could strengthen them. And it might be that the Lord's stern law was for men alone.

Now a rabbit came out of a wild raspberry patch – some were ripe this morning, he would set Mary to picking them. The rabbit sat on its backside, long ears pricked, it did not move until James was a few feet away. They were fearless at this season, stupid with their mating urge.

James thought now of Ruth who awaited him in bed. He would not speak at once about Smith's suggestion. He would please his woman, and speak later to her.

Small Mary was playing a game with round pebbles in a dusty place before the cabin, but she pouted at him. 'I wish you and Mummy would hurry up. I want my breakfast.'

'So does that rabbit. Take it a few lettuce leaves, and you eat some too to fill those corners in your tummy until breakfast time.'

'Gosh, Daddy, you're so funny.' Mary ran to the vegetable garden, and James went in, strong with desire.

'You kept me waiting a long long time,' Ruth said, smiling. She smiled that same expectant way each morning, watching him.

'Was there a change in the Lord's pink ocean?' Ruth asked after he had thanked her for his rightful pleasure, and she had thanked him for her rightful pleasure. She waited always to ask that question.

'There was no change in the Lord's pink ocean,' James Parker said.

2

'OUR fathers were both learned people,' Ruth said at breakfast. 'Better at higher things than common farming. So we know nothing about an old practice of mixing breeds of beast which was told by her mother to that Smith woman. But . . .'

'But what?'

'I'm trying to remember what, and now I do. It was a story of my mother's, told to her by Daddy, Professor Derwent Morley, the world-renowned biologist. He said that in a small mountain country in Times Before – Switzy was its name perhaps – there were certain high valleys cut off from the outer world where the same few people bred and bred and bred together until they grew weak and sickly. Mightn't our weakling beasts be suffering the same as those people in those valleys?'

James Parker's blood grew hot. 'Hush, woman! Men are not beasts.'

'Yes, James. No, I mean. Forgive my foolishness.' Ruth finished her porridge and laid down the wooden spoon. 'Stop dreaming, child. Eat the Lord's good breakfast.'

Mary scowled. 'It isn't good,' she said. 'You burnt it, Mummy.'

'Go hungry, then.' But Mary ate again.

'I want your opinion, Ruth, if you will think sensibly.'

'We are the Lord's people. Therefore the Lord must wish us well. And the Lord knows that if the animals die, we shall surely starve. So I'm in agreement with that woman. Let's do it, James.'

'Daddy!'

'Yes, Mary?'

'I say my prayers every night and every morning, and you and Mummy keep promising to tell me exactly how the Lord's pink ocean happened, but you haven't yet.'

'I will,' James Parker said. 'Now help your Mummy with the dishes, and then it's lesson time, and then there are raspberries to pick.'

'I never have any fun,' Mary said. 'Not ever. Couldn't I come with you when you trade animals with those Smiths?'

'Be a good girl, and we'll see,' James said. He went to the door, pausing there, his back to them, and he asked the question lightly: 'Ruth!' he said. 'Did you hear a sound in the night?'

'*What sound*?' Her voice was anxious.

'Not important – something like the rolling down of stones and earth on the dead hills beyond us.'

'Oh, that,' she said. 'We hear that often. No, I didn't. Did you?'

'It must have been a dream of mine,' he said, going out. He hailed Smith, and then paddled the birchbark canoe to meet him at No-Man's-Island midway across the lake. They agreed upon the exchange of livestock for that afternoon.

When James Parker reached home again, he knocked the weakling calf on the head, cleaned it, buried the entrails, and skinned a wretched bag of bones fit for nothing but the stew-pot.

After that, he went weeding among vegetables. The day had become hot, and bumble bees were busy all around him. James had never known his father, but his mother said that Daddy was a botanist, a man who understood the plants, and that he used to say: *Thank the Lord for our humble bumble bees who stay near home, passing life from flower to flower. The honey bees flew outside to die.*

But his mother could not explain such things very well because she herself had had only what she called a Fifth Grade education. It was the same with Ruth, whose father was a famous biologist, which meant a student of life, and her mother a longshoreman's beautiful daughter. So, after their two fathers were killed, their mothers could quote the sayings of their fathers, but could teach only as far as they themselves understood.

'I know I'm ignorant,' James said at his weeding. 'But I'm as good a farmer as an honest plain-ignorant man may be.'

'You're not plain-ignorant, but wise.' It was his good woman, come to join him. 'That Smith now, he's both ignorant and dishonest.'

'Dishonest? Oh, come on, Ruth!'

'Isn't it dishonest every winter to sponge on us? To borrow, he says, but does he ever repay? Oats, straw, hay, potatoes, turnips – each winter they gobble up their own, then take from us, those good-for-nothings.'

'Ruth,' James said. 'We must live in peace. Didn't our mothers tell us that?'

Ruth sighed. 'Yes, but I forget. And worry makes me say foolish things. Mary is being so difficult. I had to take the strap to her again this morning for skimping homework. Aren't these weeds just terrible?'

'I wish our carrots would grow like our weeds.'

Ruth laughed. 'My funny man.'

'The child is lonely,' James said, starting on a row of beets. 'It isn't natural for a child of nine to have only her parents for companions.'

'The Lord knows we've done our honest best for three quarters of every moon, year in, year out. And if I'm to be a woman ageing as my mother did, not many years remain to me.'

'It's the same with those Smiths,' James said. 'They try all the time, he told me. But Smith thinks as I do, that until the Lord again wills a change . . .' He did not finish because he feared to provoke the Lord. But the Lord's pink ocean had changed nine moons before babies were born on both sides of the lake.

'The beasts still mate with result, bad as it is.'

'We aren't beasts of the field,' James said in rebuke.

'Forgive my foolishness,' Ruth said.

'You are hasty in your nature, just as Mary is. But you're a wise woman when you stop to think.'

'Thank you, James.' They weeded on. It was hot now, and sweat glistened on their bodies. 'James,' she said, still weeding. 'I've stopped to think, and my thought is this: Would it be so wrong if the children were to play together?'

'It would be wrong. It's the most ancient law, coming from Times Before. They are not our kind of people.'

'But, James, these are small children, not yet people. Wouldn't it be better that they should have some fun and games together, strictly supervised – wouldn't that be better than that Smith boy climbing out of the valley? And Mary wanders too. Only yesterday I caught her up near the barricade in the West Ravine. She said she was visiting her friend the woodchuck, but I know better. Loneliness, James, it makes for mischief. We have made one great decision already today, and we're to have a rare meeting with those Smiths. Why not discuss this too?'

'Smith is worried about his boy. The *laddie*, he calls him in that barbarous speech. But the Lord . . .'

'The Lord looks with a kindly eye upon innocents. Our mothers taught us that, eh, James?'

James sighed. It was proving to be a most difficult day. 'If there is a chance for woman's talk, you could mention our Mary's loneliness, and she might respond. But don't let a suggestion come from us.'

'You're so wise, James. Now I must put the dinner on. Then let's have a nice cool swim.'

'I got a whole box, Daddy, see! And I didn't eat hardly any myself.'

'You're a good girl,' he said, and so she was. He patted her dark head. 'Mary,' he said on the way to the shore. 'Mummy tells me you were up near the barricade in the West Ravine again.'

'I was only seeing my friend, the Woodchuck. We talk together, and I give him oatcakes, and I think it's stinking of Mummy to tell on me.'

'Never use that word *stinking*, least of all about Mummy. She had to tell on you because there is terrible danger beyond the West Ravine. There is only death outside our valley. How many times am I to say that, Mary?'

'Like the stiff dead rabbit or the frozen chickadee. Like them, Daddy?'

'Yes,' he said. 'You must promise me not to go there, Mary.'

'Okay, promise.' But James Parker observed that his daughter crossed two fingers, adorable minx. They took off their loincloths and waded in, cool pure water round the ankles. 'Do you think you started my baby brother this morning in Mummy?'

'I hope so,' he said. 'But we shouldn't hope too much.'

'You're terrific, Daddy. I love it when the whole cabin shakes.'

Ruth joined them, and they swam at noon, the sun standing high above the falls. James and Ruth had both had watches once, but they were long since broken.

The sun dried them; and it was time for Ruth's vegetable stew, and for Mary's raspberries with a spoonful each of maple syrup, but no cream.

Then it was time to dress in their better clothes for the

meeting, then to put a halter on their Ayrshire bull, he was a sad head-hanging beast; and the same for their Merino ram, which was as bad. Sheep would not breed until the fall, but a change even to Smith pasture might be beneficial to the ram. Lastly, James caught the Barred Rock rooster which gave one squawk as its legs were tied.

James led the way with the bull, and Ruth followed with the ram, and Mary came third, rooster upside down on the end of a string hanging down her back. The meeting place was at the head of the lake where the inlet tumbled in.

James removed three poles from the snake-fence, his fence on his side of the brook. *Good fences make good neighbours,* his mother had told him. There was no fence on Smith's side of the inlet.

'Cross over the burrn if you have the mind,' said that man, as if granting a favour.

James growled, but under his breath. He took the bull through the fence, and motioned to Ruth and Mary to join him. Thus, Smiths and Parkers faced one another across the brook or burn, their boundary – men and bulls, women and rams, children and roosters.

It was a time to consider the exchange, a chance to reconsider it. But James Parker admitted to himself that Smith's Angus bull and Cheviot ram and Rhode Island cock were no worse beasts than his own, all as bad as beasts could be. And he admitted to himself that his human neighbours were a sturdy breed. His eyes did not dwell upon Smith, a man for whom he usually felt dislike. But in considering the ram, the edge of his glance passed over Smith's carrot-headed woman, broad of shoulder, mighty of bosom, strong as a healthy cow. The boy was fair-haired of a colour between his parents, tall for his age, a bold-eyed kid.

'Neighbour,' James Parker said. 'Let's hope that this swop bears fruit, for our beasts are terrible.' He was an honest chap.

Robert Smith laughed heartily enough to drown the babble of the brook. 'Ay, that's the truth of it,' he said.

They were men far different, but neither was a fool. Both knew that this desperate experiment, the mixing of the blood, must seem to begin with good will, or the bad blood between themselves would certainly grow worse. They therefore led their hangdog bulls apart and made farmers' talk concerning crops and weather. This left their women with a similar duty concerning the limited recipes at their disposal, and from that to the children's appetites, and from that to disobedience.

'Ian's into mischief all the time. But you can't blame a laddie.'

'Mary is the same,' Ruth said. 'It's loneliness, I think, but they are listening to us.'

Both women turned to wave their little ones away.

Mary Parker faced Ian Smith across the brook. They stared for a long time while the water tumbled merrily, and their mothers gabbled on.

'Hi, Whitey boy!' said Mary Parker.

'Hi, Nigger lassie!' said Ian Smith, and they went on staring. 'You're skinny,' he said. 'Nae bubs on ye.'

'Just a tiny acorn back of your kilt, I bet.'

That was all even, and that was funny. They put down their roosters. 'Let's play a game,' said Ian Smith, his face bright red with laughing.

'I know,' she said. 'We'll race two sticks.'

They found sticks and raced them down the brook from run to run from pool to pool. Mary won the first race, and Ian won the second. They went up to get their roosters.

'At this age, a wee bit of innocent fun and games, there would be no harm to it, I'm thinking.'

'Under strict supervision,' James Parker said, 'there would be no harm at their present age. The women could take turns to see fair play.'

So it was agreed, and the exchange of fowls and beasts was made. 'In all our days, there has never been a day like this,' James said, going home. 'It's been perhaps a bit too much.'

'But for the best,' Ruth said. She had sent Mary on to free their new old rooster. 'You know, that woman isn't so bad when one talks with her, bold and vulgar in her speech, but not bad for a common white woman.'

'That Scotty Smith was almost human this afternoon.'

'James!'

It was a change to serious mood, he knew that anxious voice. 'Yes?'

'Why did you lie to me and say that the sound in the night was a dream of yours?'

'*Lie* to you?' he said, freeing his right hand from the halter rope.

'Not lie, I mean,' she said hastily.

'I didn't want you to fear for no reason.'

'It was a long long sound, the Smith woman said, more like the buzzing of many bumble bees than the rolling down of stones and earth.'

'It was nothing but a fancy of that woman's ears.'

'Perhaps, but bumble bees don't buzz in the night.'

Strange sounds brought fear to them in the valley.

3

'THERE was a madness in those days,' he said. 'In those days men went for picnics to the moon. Don't be so impatient, child. Give the trout time to hook itself.'

'Fishing's stupid,' Mary said.

'You won't think fishing's stupid when you're eating delicious trout for breakfast.' James caught another. That made five fat trout of half a pound. They were drifting slowly beside No-Man's-Island.

'Go on about the crazy people, Daddy.'

'In those days they had flying machines and motor cars. In fact, it was my father's Cadillac machine that saved the day at the West Ravine. You will have noticed its vast hulk still there.'

'Yes, Daddy. How, though, saved the day?'

'Because it barred entry to the wicked people who were trying to attack, and your grand-daddies shot them with bullets one by one until all were dead, excepting a last enemy woman who shot both your grand-daddies, it was such bad luck, and then my mother took the gun and shot that female with the very last shell in our possession.'

'How old were you then, Daddy?'

'I was four, and Mummy was two. I remember big bangs, but that is all I can remember.'

'What are big bangs?'

'Great sounds like thunder, Mary.'

'I hate thunder.'

'It is the voice of the Lord's displeasure.' There were black clouds in the North this evening, above the head of the valley whence came the bountiful spring that nourished their lake.

'Got one!' Mary screamed.

'Sit still, child. You'll upset the canoe.'

'I love fishing,' Mary said when he had killed her trout and baited again with a ruddy worm from the manure pile.

'. . . That's eight we have now, enough for a hearty breakfast.' James paddled slowly home. It was very still on the lake, and thunder muttered.

'Horrid thunder,' Mary said. 'Perhaps the Lord is angry with us for trading those beasts lately.'

'Continuing our story,' James said, to keep her mind and his off the grumble of the Lord's displeasure. 'In those days they had many things, not only flying machines and motor cars, but workhorse vehicles snorting on the farm; and perhaps the strangest power of all, called the electric, for cooking, lighting, even heating, for the radios they listened with, and the televisions they saw with. But you have seen the wreckage of such things in our junkpile'

'Those queer boxes, yes. What did they see with them, Daddy?'

'They saw about smelly breath and body odours, my mother always said.'

'Ian smells, and I told him so. I told him his legs were all cowdung and it was time he had a real good wash.'

'And what did he say?'

'He just laughed, and said I smell too because I'm a nigger lassie. Ian's fun.'

'H'mm. They had many powers, but there was a madness in those days. Perhaps all the powers they had were what made the madness in them, who can tell, but so my mother said my father told her. He said that for many years while they were doing their best to banish body smells and wash their undergarments white as snow, they were doing their best to stink up the air, the land, the rivers, the oceans.'

'You said never to say stinking, Daddy.'

'I am explaining why, dear child. They made a stink-hole of the world until at last the Lord's patience was exhausted, and the Lord struck overnight. Now, Mary, you will understand that all we know came to us from our mothers, who were fine ignorant women. Mine used to say that like many another great man before him, my father did not take his woman for her brains, he took her for his bed.'

'It could be the same the other way round,' Mary said. 'I wouldn't want to take a man all brains, Daddy. I would want a terrific man like you.'

'Thank you, Mary. Now pay attention. It happened that our parents, Mummy's and mine, had driven with the Cadillac and trailer from a city called Boston where millions of people lived and poisoned one another; and they came to this one high gem of a lake, still unspoiled amid filth and stench and broken bottles knee-deep along every highway ditch. The owner of our side of the valley was a rich summer visitor, what was called a hobby farmer, seemingly quite a decent whitey who, as soon as he knew my father's learned occupation, said that they could certainly camp here for a while if my father would make for him a study of the plant life by the lake.

'On the other shore lived the Smith family, common working farmers, and beyond them, just over those cliffs, were the MacDonald people. Old Smith had also sold several small lots for cottages by the lake where people could escape the filth of the lower land and the ocean shore.

'It happened that on the night the Lord chose to strike, the MacDonald man and woman had crossed over by the bridle path to have an unbridled party with the Smith man and woman.'

'Did those common men trade women like our bulls have traded heifers, Daddy?'

'I don't know, Mary. It would not surprise me. Thus it was, if our mothers' counts were accurate, that sixteen white citizens and four black citizens chanced to be here on that fateful night. I was not born until a month afterwards, and Mummy two years later.'

Thunder rumbled to the North, and clouds were inky black in sunlight. 'I'm scared, Daddy. Couldn't you please hurry up and tell me before the Lord gets really cross?'

James paddled more strongly. 'The evening before, our people had walked down to the falls to see from this purity to the usual black oil and muddy cream and soapsuds where once there had been a clean river and a clear blue ocean. But on the fateful morning they were awakened by strange sounds and mighty clamour from the direction of the town – motor horns, gunshots, hooters, wailing sirens, a fearful racket my mother called it, and all hastened to the falls to look.

'What they saw was a pink river far below, and beyond that a pink ocean all the way to the edge of the world, and motor cars dashing hither and thither in the town to crash and smash, and distant screams, it was a madness. And then as suddenly all was still.

'It was your mother's father, Professor Derwent Morley of Boston U, a man wise about all life, who raised his right hand then and cried: THE GREAT LORD ALGA HAS STRUCK AT LAST, and all the others from both sides of the lake cried after him: *The Great Lord Alga*. But his was the first voice, and he was the Lord's interpreter.'

'Please, Daddy, get a move on.'

'I've nearly finished. Suffice to say that after a few days, food ran short here at the lake, and so did the various oils and gases from the earth that they used for their cooking and their motor

cars and for many other purposes. And down there was a town
with such materials in abundance.

'The town was dead, and the Lord's pink ocean was still a
lively pink, but the foolish ones decided to risk it, strictly
against the advice of those wise scholars, our two fathers. All
but our people, and the rich white man, and the Smiths and
MacDonalds – who were still engaged in the same drunken
orgy – all drove down to the town and perished.

'The next occurrence was that the seemingly decent white
man and rich hobby farmer, fearing for the needs of his own
fat stomach and that of a woman so-called secretary, showed
his true colours and ordered us black people out of the valley.
It was necessary therefore to deal with them.' James Parker
coughed. He did not like recounting this tale of terror to
a child with Mary's vivid imagination, but she should know
such truths lest she become too friendly with her new playmate.

'Serve him right, the pig. You said that the foolish people all
perished, Daddy. But what happened when your two fathers
were killed?'

'That was four years later. There must have been a pocket of
survivors somewhere among the hills. At any rate criminals
tried to fight their way into our valley. But we and the Smiths
and the MacDonalds won the day, losing all our brave fighting
men in that last action. Only the mothers and children remained.'

'And there is no one but us anywhere now, Daddy?'

'There is no one but us,' he said. 'I have been many times
to the head of the valley to the very highest point where our
pure springs emerge, and I have looked far and wide, Mary,
and everywhere I see live pink water and grey death. There is
no one but us.'

'Why us, though, Daddy?'

'You mean, why do we survive? That was explained by

your Mummy's father to his woman. He said that the water of this lake comes from the deep bowels of the earth, and by a miracle stayed pure. The other reason that we remain safe is that our waterfall skips and splashes from ledge to ledge, and thus is broken in its fall. No other streams come in from outside our valley, and thus we are protected from the Lord's pink punishment which cannot climb to us.'

'And how did the Lord make the ocean pink?'

'With a mass of tiny living plants that grow and eat the filth and die themselves and are born again to eat again.'

James grounded the canoe, and they went ashore. A first wind stirred the trees and lightning flickered beyond the steep places of which he had spoken.

'There might be other people somewhere, Daddy. I know Mummy is afraid of that. But why is she afraid? I don't quite see.'

'Because if there were people, they would try to come into our rich green valley, just as the wicked survivors tried long ago, and there is not food enough for more than our family and those Smiths.'

'But the bad people couldn't reach here because they would die on the way,' Mary said. 'Unless . . .' She stopped and looked up at the sky. Thunder was much louder, crackling above the hilltops. 'The Lord is coming to punish us,' she said, and ran for the cabin.

James Parker wondered whether Mary had guessed their fear that the droning sound heard by night might have been a flying machine of wicked men.

The lightning was bright, and the first drops of rain were falling as he closed the hens in. Raccoons came hunting every night, but he could not trap them either by snare or deadfall. If he ever failed to shut that door, the cunning kill-lusting devils would murder every hen and the cockerel too. It was one of the many tasks that an ignorant farmer dare not forget.

He had forgotten once, but had heard the commotion in time to save half the flock. 'We live always with danger,' James Parker said, his voice silenced by the voice of the Lord's displeasure. He had collected two more eggs, and that made twelve, and some should be fertile because the Rhode Island rooster had been treading his females with unexpected vigour. Tomorrow he would set them to the broody hen.

'Don't be afraid,' he said to his womenfolk in the cabin. It was a short and mighty storm, and it passed down South to the Lord's pink ocean.

'Mummy, you said there used to be story books. Why do we have no story books any more?'

'Because those stupid Smiths burned them up. Daddy will explain.'

'It was in the year before you were born, at the end of winter when snow was gone from open ground but still deep in the woods. I remember that morning all too well. I made my dawn pilgrimage to the waterfall, and to my astonishment I saw that the Lord's pink ocean was a battleground of pink and blue.

'Greatly rejoicing, I came back to the old house to tell your mother, and to bed with her. It was on that morning, so we think, that you began life's journey.

'Suddenly smelling smoke, I dashed outside, and what did I see? I saw that Smith had lit a great bonfire by the waterfall in celebration. I raced to warn the fool of danger, but I had not run many paces from the house when I saw it happen. A gust of wind jumped the fire over the waterfall, and in a moment dried winter grass was blazing on both shores of the lake.

'Your mother and I had time only to save a few essential tools, this table, those two chairs, and mugs and plates and spoons, some sheepskins, and throw them into shallow water and throw ourselves in also, when the grassfire roared upon us.

Pay heed to my words, young lady, there is no such racing danger as a grassfire after winter.

'The old house burned down, and with it went our few story books and other inessential things. Those Smiths suffered likewise.'

'And did they ever say one word of regret or do one extra stroke of work to make up for what was their stupid fault entirely?'

'Hush, Ruth! Didn't the Lord punish them, and us innocent ones too, by that very day sending back the Lord's pink ocean?'

'It wasn't Ian's fault. Ian wasn't alive except perhaps just starting like me inside his Mummy.'

'Quite right, Mary. And things could have been worse. Our own lives were spared. Our livestock, being on higher pasture where the grass was short, were spared, as also the forest deep in snow, the haybarn too.

'But what a time of toil lay ahead. Not only the usual crops to plant and tend and harvest, but many trees to fell, and this cabin to build and chink with moss before winter was again upon us, and your Mummy increasingly pregnant, although she did her manful best. Yet we survived, Mary, and you were born in this cozy cabin.'

'It's too bad about the story books, though, Daddy.'

'Not so bad perhaps, because many were almost entirely beyond our comprehension. There was one, I remember, about something called Nuclear Fission. I understood hardly a word of it except the articles, auxiliary verbs, conjunctions and the like. The real tragedy is that our scholarly fathers were not spared to educate us. As it is, Mummy and I have only a thorough knowledge of the three R's of plain ignorance, and that is all that we can teach to you. What are you writing, Mary, on that piece of birchbark with soot from our cabin stove?'

'I'm writing a story for Ian, and Ian is writing a story for me, so we can both have story books.'

'What are the stories about, my girl?'

'Secret,' Mary said.

'It's long past your bedtime,' said her Mummy.

4

THE oats ripened soon, and there were long hours and days of scything, thrashing, winnowing. Life was labour, with a slow satisfaction to it. Potatoes and common vegetables dug and stored, apples picked, it was time then for James to yoke the pair of oxen and to plough his land. That was a long business, his beasts weedy, his ploughshare worn but he had no other.

After ploughing, they had a holiday to give thanks for the Lord's good harvest. That one day of late sleeping and oi thanksgiving feast (but it was a scrawny fowl that even Ruth's skill could not make tender); then James began on his winter's work.

He felled a first birch up there in the hardwood glade, limbed it, saving every precious piece of wood. Soon Ruth would come, and they would saw it into firewood lengths. 'According to the notches on the giant sugar maple,' James Parker said, alone in the forest, 'four cut by my father, six cut by my mother, all the rest cut by me, I'm now a man of forty-four, and already I tire more easily and I have no strapping son. What will happen to the women when I grow old and feeble?' It was an anxiety that bothered him from time to time; but here came his good woman, and they went to work.

That winter was long and cold, and they felt the chill increasingly because their tired sheepskins were losing fleece. But it was a good winter for working in the woods, the snow not being too deep. And the children were much happier now that they were allowed to play together. They found strips of shiny metal from a thing called a refrigerator in the junkpile. With these for runners, James fashioned a sled. He had good fun trying it out with Ruth, she giggled like a girl again. Then the children packed a run to the lake and shovelled snow down to bare ice, and they could slide nearly as far as No-Man's-Island, to which neither Parkers nor Smiths laid claim. It was a pleasure to see and hear the children happy, kept out of mischief, away from the deadly dangers that surrounded them.

James finished cutting the year's supply of firewood, and moved farther up his side of the valley to evergreen forest where he began to thin a cedar grove for fence poles, and to cut some spruce logs which he would use to make the new hen-house. Of the twenty-two chickens that had hatched by the time leaves were falling, twelve were pullets, ten were cockerels, and all were healthy, a remarkable improvement.

The snow was still deep up here at the valley's head, not far below the gushing spring, and the sun was so warm that he removed his outer sheepskin coat. He could hear his neighbour's axe across the brook. Parker chopped steadily. Smith chopped by fits and starts.

Then James Parker stopped chopping altogether, and there was silence too across the way.

The reason that James stopped was that he heard a sound, unmistakably a sound, a droning like that described by the Smith woman last summer. It was over in the East, and moving from North to South, growing, still growing, no longer growing, fading, soon gone altogether over the Lord's pink ocean.

James dropped his axe and ran up beside the brook. He climbed the narrowing valley to the very head, which was bare of trees, and a man could see in all directions. His neighbour arrived. Both panted, but their breathing eased, and the only sound then was the healthy burble of the spring.

'You heard it, Neighbour?'

'I heard it, Neighbour.'

James turned slowly, searching the flat circle of the world, and Smith did likewise. There was nothing to be seen but the Lord's pink ocean and the dead land under snow.

'There!' said James Parker.

'Ay, there!' said Robert Smith. They pointed in the same direction, to the South and West this time, to the right of the lake below them. The droning, the buzzing of the bumble bees, grew again, was steady again, was dwindling again. It died altogether to the North.

'I saw nothing.'

'Nor me neither.'

'If we could not see it, then it could not see us.'

'Not without it had one of them televisions.'

'It could have some such thing. We know so little.'

'That's right,' said Robert Smith. 'The woman will have heard it, and be feared.'

'My woman also will be afraid.'

'We could tell them it was nothing.'

'Not even women would believe that nothing passed us to one side, and then nothing passed us to the other.'

'That's right,' said Robert Smith again. They walked down, each on his own side of the brook. Smith stopped, and so did Parker.

'What should we do if one o' them flying machines ever comes? You have a good head on you, Neighbour. What's your opinion what to do?'

James was pleased at this compliment. He felt friendly to Smith, and gave thought to a most worrying problem. 'We couldn't hide,' he said. 'If we hid, they would find the evidence of our beasts and buildings, and would hunt us down. We have no guns for self-defence, nothing but our bows and arrows, knives and axes, and what good would they do against the bullets our mothers spoke of? My considered opinion is that we should put out the welcome mat.'

'I'm with you, Neighbour. That's the best chance we have.'

They discussed the matter further as good neighbours should, and then went on down to their evergreen woods. Robert Smith said that he was felling tamarack, a tough slow business with the axe, but his woman was keeping a watchful eye upon the ewes which might begin lambing even today . . .

'I will gladly help you,' James Parker said, responding to the hint, and he did, taking one end of Smith's crosscut saw. He gave Robert Smith three hours of honest labour, and Smith promised to do the same for him tomorrow, but arrived late and gave one hour only.

It was the same ancient story. James had found out long ago that two men working together achieved more than twice as much as those two men working alone. But Smith always took more than he gave, and so Parker always went back to working alone. However, as he kept telling his headstrong woman, the most important thing was to live in peace, or they would not live at all.

But their relations were on the whole better as winter yielded to spring and it was time again to work the land. They heard no more strange sounds by day or night, and that fear dwindled. It was a season of blessings, for the crossbred lambs were sturdy beasts, and so were the crossbred calves, and the first young cockerel was delicious eating, and the children were happy at their fun and games.

Thus, another summer came, the forty-fifth summer of James Parker's life, and perhaps the best were it not for one thing – try as he might, with all the lusty vigour of an outdoorsman, he could not get his woman pregnant. She is barren, he thought. It's all her fault. But he did not say that.

It was Mary who made the suggestion: 'Ian and me were saying this morning – it was after we'd finished racing sticks in the brook, which was terrific fun because it's much bigger after that rain last night – well, we were saying that we've never ever yet been allowed to have a feast together. So we just thought what fun it would be to kill a fatted lamb at No-Man's-Island and make a huge fire and cook it whole, and then us three Parkers and those three Smiths would all have a feast.'

'But they're not our kind of people. Never in our lives have we broken bread together.'

'It isn't bread I'm talking about, Daddy stupid. It's roast fatted lamb.'

'Don't call your wise father stupid, Mary, or I shall have to take the strap to you again.'

'To break bread together is an expression my mother taught me, meaning only to eat in company, so mind your manners, Mary.'

'Sorry, Daddy, I didn't mean it. Well, Ian said he would pop the question to his dad and mum, so I said I would pop it too.'

'Your opinion, Ruth?'

'For myself, I don't want to break bread with those people, but if it would give the children pleasure, I personally would not object. Also, James . . .'

'Speak up, woman.'

'James, I know you hold tradition dear, but mightn't such a friendly gesture as a joint sacrifice and feast with those people meet with the Lord's approval?'

James frowned, considering this. Another thing his mother had said to him was: *James, beware the thin end of the wedge.* 'I can hear that Smith hailing you,' said Ruth.

They met at the bridge, and both faced the Lord's pink ocean.

'No change, Neighbour.'

'No change, Neighbour.'

'This suggestion of the kids', are you against it?'

'I think not,' James said. 'It would be in keeping with our good neighbour policy, and also a token of thanks for the success of our cross-breeding policy.'

'Ay, and an economy too, one strong lamb's a good feast for six.'

'That's agreed, then, but whose lamb?'

'We could spin the medal for it.' Smith produced that medal from his breeches pocket. 'My mum said they used to call heads and tails in the days o' siller.'

'My mother also spoke of that custom. There are no heads and tails on this coin, though.'

'No. Just the one side with words, and the other plain.'

'If we tossed here, we might lose your medal in the water. Step on to my land. Do by all means.'

'Ta,' said Smith, and did so. 'It's too big for a right spin, but I'll do my best. Words up, your lamb. Words down, my lamb. Here goes.' He made a clumsy toss, words up. The medal did not spin at all and therefore landed on James Parker's good green grass, words up. 'Your lamb,' said Smith with satisfaction.

'You ch . . .,' James began, but he stopped himself from the fighting word.

'What was that you were after saying?'

'You chanced to win,' James said, his anger under control. 'Very well,' he said. 'I shall bring my lamb tomorrow to No-Man's-Island. It will be your responsibility to light the fire early and have good cooking embers by the time the sun stands over this waterfall. No good embers, no free lamb. May the Lord go with you, Neighbour.'

Smith grunted, strode across the bridge, and slammed shut his livestock gate. James Parker had been cheated, but he was inclined to think that he had got the better of that uncouth trickster.

5

THE feasting place on No-Man's-Island was a flat rock, facing down the lake to the waterfall. Robert Smith had done a decent job for once, building the fire of apple logs, now burned down to perfect cooking embers.

By right of ownership James Parker had said the words: 'Lord, we offer this lamb,' bled it, skinned it, cleaned it, and hung it from tall stakes by lengths of that old electric wire for which there were so many uses on the farm.

The scents of apple smoke and roasting lamb set his mouth to water. 'Nearly ready, would you agree?' he said with a formality befitting the occasion.

'We should mebbe turn it the once more,' said Smith politely.

They turned the sizzling roast. 'It sure does smell yummy,' Mary said from the shore nearby. 'Dead man's choke,' she said, throwing a long pebble up and out, but it made a big splash, no dead man's choke.

'Wee bezzom, yon was awfy,' said her playmate in his awful accent.

'Mind yer manners, Ian,' said his mum.

But now the time had positively come. The children were summoned, and James Parker put a final razor sharpness to his carving knife, and the sun stood high above the waterfall, and a sound grew behind them from the North.

The flying machine went low along the Parker side of the valley, turned above the waterfall and flew back along the Smith side of the valley.

The Parkers and the Smiths were stricken dumb.

It was a roaring thing of a mustardy colour above the blue water of the lake. But it flew South again into the sun, gone perhaps, the sound had almost died away.

No, it was growing, changing to a higher pitch. It came low over the waterfall, almost touching, skimming, touching now, throwing up twin columns of spray from two long canoes that were its feet.

The thing sank deeper, and the roar changed to splutterings, but gathered once more as it swam towards them along the lake, ungainly creature.

The Parkers and the Smiths sat as still as graven images above a fatted lamb, their summer sacrifice and feast, roasted to perfection.

But despite their faults – the one inclined toward too much virtue, the other toward too little – they were men of spirit, and they rallied.

'The welcome mat, Robert, eh?' James Parker said.

'The welcome mat, James, it is,' said Robert Smith. Never before had they addressed one another thus familiarly.

The machine came noisily up the centre of the lake, headed for them on the only island. James remembered from his mother's words, and from a picture in a story book before the books were all burned up, that these things pulled themselves along with a kind of spinner. Perhaps the hazy circle in front of its nose would be made by that spinner. Yes, he was right. When the machine was a short distance away, not much farther than small Mary might toss a stone, the spinner slowed its spinning, the insides coughed a last time, and were quiet. All was silence but for the lapping of small waves against the twin canoes.

Then a door opened in the side, and a man sprang down to stand on one canoe. Blessed relief, his hands were empty. He was a short square man with a very broad grin and cheeks red as maples in the fall. He wore baggy pants made from some grey cloth, a sacklike jerkin of the same, and a strange white band thing round his neck. There was someone else in the machine, for a rope was handed down, but that someone did not yet emerge.

The man coiled the rope and threw one end deftly. He was much quicker and neater in his movements than were the lumbering Smiths and Parkers. James had time only for these few thoughts before he and Smith were hauling on the rope.

'Let's tie one end to *that* tree,' the man said, 'and secure both floats, and the other end to *that* tree, and there we are, all ship-shape, grounded on the beach.' He laughed, seemingly a merry fellow, stepped ashore below the sizzling lamb, and turned to give a hand to the other person, who was still smaller, dressed a little differently, with cheeks like smiling McIntosh apples.

'I am the Reverend Noel Avakana,' said the man, 'and this is my wife, Martha. We bring the word of our dear Lord Jesus.' He made a queer sign with his hand, from brow down to belly button, then across his broad chest.

'I am James Parker, and this is my woman, Ruth, and this is our child, Mary. Welcome, strangers.' Parker raised his right hand in the Lord's own sign.

'I am Robert Smith, and this is my woman, Janet, and this is our laddie, Ian. Welcome strangers.' Smith raised his right hand in the Lord's own sign.

'You're just in time to share our feast.'

'Ay, and very welcome.'

'But we would not dream of taking your good food from you.'

'There's a muckle dinner for a'body,' Smith said, his speech even broader than usual.

'But we have our own arctic char in the freezer in the plane. No, I insist. Martha, pray fetch us a morsel of *irkalukpik*.' Martha Avakana bounded nimbly aboard, and as nimbly ashore with a piece of fish, which he divided. 'An appetizer,' he said, laughing, but became serious: 'Dear Lord Jesus, bless our food.'

'Bless our food, Lord,' they said.

'Who's this Jesus?'

'Hush, Mary.'

They ate the raw fish, which was very good, crumbling coldly in the mouth. Then eight people feasted on that sturdy lamb; and then they talked in the afternoon.

'. . . You flew from up there. But where is up there?'

'Nearly two thousand miles to the North, Mr Parker. Now in July our ice is breaking, and now spring flowers make our land a glorious carpet of colour. You see, good people, the waters up there are ever cold; hence the pink armies of algae could not reach us. We were spared by the mercy of our Lord, just as you were spared.'

'Did you know that we were here?'

'Our people knew in the early days, forty years ago and long before my time, when spying satellites in polar orbit still photographed the Earth, relaying to our Greenland station. We knew of small colonies of scientific chaps in the Antarctic – few ladies there, alas. We knew of quite numerous survivors across the Pole in Siberia. But the photographic systems in those satellites failed one by one. And so, as I said, for some forty years we had no news of your fate.

'It was towards the end of my father's life – he was the Anglican Bishop, Peter of the Arctic – that he sent for me and said: *Noel, there is a possibility that they survive, and if they survive, it must be in heathen sin. Therefore, now that you are an ordained priest, I have decided to make them your prime evangelizing task, and to entrust to you the Mission plane. Do not breathe a word, lest those Catholics hear.* And so for years now, Martha and I have been caching gasoline and supplies, gradually extending our range southwards, hunting you down, one might say.'

The priest giggled to himself. 'It was last summer at about this time that we reached far enough for a first thermal contact.'

'*Thermal*? We are ignorant people.'

'Yes, I'm sorry. I mean that with heat-recording instruments we picked up a positive reaction, an indication of two separate fires from this very place, quite enough to whet our appetites, but we were short of fuel. By this spring we had made further stocks along the way, and undertook another reconnaissance flight.'

'We heard you,' Smith said bluntly. 'Why didn't you come for a look?'

'Because, Mr Smith, we were on skis and feared that the ice would not bear us so late in your season. Also, we didn't like to buzz you in order to make quite certain, lest you might take us for enemies.'

Smith and Parker exchanged quick glances, but small Mary was speaking: 'Reverend, were there many people in the world in Times Before?'

'Very many, Mary. More people than a girl could count if she spent her whole life counting them. And of those billions, seven eighths were starving, and one eighth burned up their surplus food, do not ask me why.' Noel Avakana frowned and then laughed merrily. 'Why, only this morning we flew over the great dead city of Montreal where once three million rich people lived and hated with many bombs. Ladies and gentlemen, we would have run you to earth long ago had the preparations not been so difficult and dangerous. We had to find safe lakes all the way from the Arctic Ocean.'

'If there are other safe lakes, why no folk at them?'

'Because, Ian, my dear boy, the lakes of the Canadian Shield were almost all without people, even in Times Before, and only one in fifty thousand is a blue lake now. But that is a good question, Ian.'

'Are there many people like us, black people and white people up there? Or are they all pudding faces?'

'There were many white oilmen and soldier families at the beginning, Mary, and some black oilmen and black soldier families too, but they could not seem to settle in our beautiful North, and many of those foolish virgins grew desperate and flew out to certain death. It was sad, indeed. There are some of you Southern people still, and fine citizens among them. I would mention one only, a brilliant young man named Curtis George. But all are not suited to our lovely cold world. By which I do not mean to imply that your world down here is not beautiful and bountiful. What wouldn't we give for a few lambs as tender as the one we have just eaten, much better than blubbery seal, I must admit, eh, Martha?'

'Yes, Noel, not for every day, but Sunday lunch perhaps.' Martha Avakana giggled. 'But it's nice here. It would make an ideal rest camp for our people to come to at the awkward seasons – just before break-up, say, in late June, and just before freeze-up in September. That would be lovely for our people, and so would the roast lamb.'

'Who are your people? Forgive our ignorance.'

'We are the People,' the Priest said gravely. 'The Innuit, or as you called us, the Eskimos. We are a peaceful people. We didn't make wars, nor pollute the Earth. We didn't spurn Jesus, and then drop atom bombs in the name of Jesus. We didn't send guns to kill black babies, and then starve the surviving black babies out of respect for protocol. We watched all these terrible things, and we were helpless, a few thousand Innuit above a world of Sodom and Gomorrah.'

He laughed. 'But I am making us out to be angels, which we are far from being. Indeed, we're mortal sinners like the next man. And there is no excuse for us to sprout holy wings just because our way of life didn't tempt us to pollute air and land and water. We were spared those pitfalls. Nor was it through any virtue of ours that the ocean at home never rises to thirty-five degrees Fahrenheit, the critical point for the pink algae army.' He looked serious again. 'Yet, what happens is ordained. It was ordained that we should survive, and that you, dear friends, should survive, and that those few others should survive. It is for us to bear the torch.'

'What is it like up there at home, I can't quite see it?'

'You will, Mary dear. I'll make sure you do. But how can I describe the wonders of our hard cold world where, for all their faults, men live at peace; where we can grow no trees or crops; where we cannot keep fat cattle and sheep such as yours, unless we were lucky enough to have some in the deep freeze. It is a land where we never kill for fun, but a land where we must kill to live.'

'Does that mean you eat one another?' Ian asked.

'My goodness gracious, dear Lord, Ian, no. Oh, no no no. Well, if I am to be entirely honest with you, I have to admit that there have been cases in extreme hunger, but they are few and very very far between.'

'You said before that it's always night in wintertime. What do you do, just fly around in the dark?'

'No, Mary. With the limited landing aids at our disposal, we restrict our flying to mercy missions. What do we do in the long nights of winter? I will tell you, dear. We study the Holy Bible – I have copies for you – and we worship our dear Lord Jesus. In those terrible times before when the world turned to Mammon, we turned to Jesus, our Strength and our Redeemer.'

'Who's this Jesus?'

'Patience, my child, I will explain.'

Noel Avakana beamed, and then looked serious or even sad. Both he and Martha looked serious or even sad whenever they stopped smiling, which was not often. They also looked very hot, sweat pouring down their brown-red faces, and down inside their funny clothes perhaps. But the day was not hot, in fact pleasantly cool here in the shade of an old white pine.

'You both look simply boiling,' Mary said. 'Why not take off your clothes and have a swim?'

'Take off . . . – the very idea!'

'Hush, Martha. Remember that these are untutored savages.'

He looked at the savages one by one, and his beady eyes were gleaming, and he said: 'In your lonely exile you have been deprived of the Church's blessing. You have had neither instruction, nor Baptism, nor Confirmation. Also, through no fault of your own, you elders have been living in sin against our Lord's commandments, thus your sweet innocents are unwitting bastards.'

James Parker was puzzled, but he listened to the small earnest man, to whom it would be unwise to show that one took offence.

'It is for these reasons that I am come: First, to accord you the rites and blessings of the Church. Thereafter to offer you Christian counsel. You are free, of course, entirely free to decide about these matters. Therefore please discuss them among yourselves.'

The families went apart. 'What's this Jesus and this Christian, all this blessings guff?'

'Hold your tongue, Mary.' But Ruth continued: 'I remember my mother telling me about some such thing, it was a sort of joke.'

'Mine also, now you mention it,' said James. 'But the thing died out way back in Times Before, my mother said, and all their churches were always empty except for especially holy times like swearing to love and to cherish for ever, which meant next year, or like burying dead people. But we must win the confidence of this funny little fellow, so let's humour him.'

The Smiths had reached the same conclusion, and both

fathers politely so informed the funny little fellow, who grinned with broad pleasure. 'Martha,' he said. 'Pray fetch the garments.'

'Yes, dear.' She hastened to the flying machine and returned with three garments much like her own, bright sacks upside down with a hole to put your head through, even a small one for Mary. 'What's this for?' the irrepressible child demanded.

'The Mother Hubbard is for decency,' he said gravely. 'An Anglican female of any age should at all times be decently covered top and bottom.'

Thus, for the first time, except against cold, were the splendid bosoms of Janet Smith and Ruth Parker decently covered.

'It must be a strange cold world up there,' James said.

'How can they give suck to their babies if it isn't decent?' Ruth enquired.

'How can they make their babies if at all times?' Mary asked.

But the Reverend Noel Avakana was now ready to administer mysterious rites, reading from a small brown book. It took a long time, and some of the things he said and the questions he asked sounded quite beautiful for a lot of heathen guff, and in the end he raised his right hand much as they raised their right hands to the Lord, and he blessed them in the name of his Lord.

'My heartiest congratulations!' he cried then joyfully, shaking hands with everyone, and so did Martha. 'Congratulations, Mr and Mrs Smith. Congratulations, Mr and Mrs Parker. Congrats, Mary. Congrats, Ian. Now, would you two young people be so good as to free our moorings?'

'But surely you will be our guests for tonight at least,' James Parker said. 'Do please stay.'

'You'll be verra welcome, Reverend.'

'Delighted, yes, delighted. How kind you are. May we camp on this lovely island, then? But there are still some hours of daylight, plenty of time for a spin. You see it is a golden opportunity, I suppose one might better say a pinken opportunity . . .' He giggled with the utmost glee. 'At any rate a heaven-sent opportunity to study the algae host out there. No one else has been so far South before. In fact, we Anglicans have kept this whole pilgrimage a secret. No secret now, though – those Holy Romans have missed the boat. And so, with your approval, we shall break the wonderful news up home, and establish this base camp. Then our scientists will be down, and delightful chaps you'll find them. On the road, Martha.'

Martha skipped aboard, and he followed, but turned on what he had called the float and said: 'Anyone want a spin?'

All six of them shook their heads.

'Later, perhaps later, when you are more used to civilized ways. And then, who knows, we could take you one at a time, or both the children, we could take you for a ride, for a long long ride to our happy hunting grounds. Now be good sports and give our floats a mighty shove. Toodle-oo, then.'

The flying machine came to noisy life and swam down the lake.

'I wouldn't go spinning in that invention of the devil,' said James Parker. 'Not if it was for life or death.'

'Nor me neither,' said Robert Smith.

They took their families home; then paddled again to No-Man's-Island for a long discussion. When the flying machine had come back, and night had fallen, and the lake was peaceful, no sound but the monotonous PONK of yellow frogs, James Parker and Robert Smith took the only course open to them. They slew the sleeping clergyman and his woman.

6

THE moon was a shining ball, giving ample illumination for their work, while a light breeze ruffled water, and frogs on marshy shores went PONK.

First they searched the flying machine. 'There's nothing of service to us, Robert.'

'Nothing, James, unless it could be these two books called Holy Bibles that funny wee chap said he brought for us. The kids are always after story books.'

'Set them aside, then. There is also this wicked gun and the box of bullets. Might they be of service, Robert, purely in self-defence?'

'Set them aside, then, and the axes. Mine are fair worn out.'

'Mine too, Robert. But that's all, I think. Everything else is fit only for the junkpile. Agreed?'

'I'm with you, James. Now for them rocks.'

They fetched heavy rocks to put inside the thing, and talked between exertions. 'He said that they came to hunt us down.'

'Ay, and he said that they would take us for a ride up North.'

'And he lusted after our beasts to steal them to that terrible deep-freeze country.'

'She said another thing: She said that our place would make an ideal rest camp, her very words. Just think of them eating up our fowls and beasts, and then us too when the wee devils got real hungry.'

'And our women, Robert, covered for decency top and bottom.'

'I like my wumman's bosoms fine. I like her altogether.'

'My feelings exactly, Robert. For what did the Lord make women if he made their bodies shameful? There, the thing will be deep enough in the water when we add the corpses.'

They each took a bloody sleeping bag and dumped it in. 'They were not our kind of people, Robert. That is the most important thing.'

'Not our kind of people, James. You've hit it on the head.'

'Our task is nearly done. There remains the question of these things we set aside. I'm not entirely happy about the story books for the children, a bad influence surely, Robert. And besides, if others of the little fellows should ever come, which the Lord forbid, might they not recognize their Holy Bibles?'

'You're right, James. Throw them in. But the axes – if we hewed ash handles, who could then know these axes from our own?'

'Let's keep the axes, Robert.'

'The gun and the box of bullets would be like a defence against attack.'

'That they would,' said James Parker.

'I could keep them right well hidden.'

'And I could keep them safe and sound.' But James was un-easy now. There was one gun only. In the soft light of the moon he could see a hardening in his neighbour's face, a dis-trust like his own. He went on carefully: 'There is the danger that they might find them, however well hidden by one of us or by both of us. I say that the danger is greater than the advantage. Let's throw these inventions of the devil in too. Agreed, Neighbour?'

'Agreed, Neighbour. Throw 'em in with the corpses and rocks and all the junk.' That was done, their old hostility again forgotten.

They pushed the heavy-laden machine off shore, boarded their canoes, and slowly towed it out with the Reverend Noel Avakana's mooring rope. There was a deep hole in the lake, perhaps bottomless, or so deep that no fishing line of theirs had ever grounded.

√ith the new steel axes, they made several gashes in the light metal floats of the flying machine, backed off smartly, and watched it sink. There were many bubbles in the quiet night, then no more bubbles.

'May the Lord let them rest in the peace they disturbed,' James Parker said.

Robert Smith spoke likewise, and then he said: 'I'm thinking that we'll need to tell this to the women. It's hard to pull the wool over the women's eyes.'

'I agree, but not the children, it would give them nightmares, not being old enough to understand such things. To the children we should simply say that those funny little people flew away in their flying machine while they were sound asleep.'

James Parker paddled home. No birds called in the night. There were no birds of night in the valley which was his home. Ruth awaited him at the shore. She was wearing her new upper garment, doubtless against the moonlit chill.

'Well, woman,' he said.

'Wife,' she said. 'I'm your wife, and I could not sleep. Why are you so late?'

'Smith and I did what we had to do. Those heathens and their inventions of the devil now rest in peace at the bottom of the lake. No trace remains.'

She glared at him. 'You fool!' she cried, stamping her bare foot. 'What fools men are. Why did you not consult me? Oh, you fool.'

He advanced on her to administer the beating she deserved, but his woman did not flinch. 'Why do you dare call me a fool?'

'Because you are one. Because if you had consulted me, I would have shown you the wisdom of even a foolish wife. You should have tampered secretly with the machine, broken a few small things like this and that . . .'

'Like which and what?'

'Listen to me! Then they would have gone for another spin tomorrow, and would have tumbled to perish in the Lord's pink ocean where no one dares to follow. But what will happen now? They will send other machines to see down into deepest water, and they will find it, and will kill us. That's why I call you a fool, and why I want no part of you, my so-called husband. Go sleep in the haybarn.' She turned and left him.

I should have flogged her on the spot, he thought, but it is late, and I'm tired after that grievous labour, in no mood for caterwauling in the cabin. Fear and the wicked influence of those people have twisted the woman's mind. I shall sleep now and straighten the woman's mind out for her in the morning.

James awoke as the sun broke from cliffs across the lake. He climbed out of his sweet-smelling bed of hay, feeling refreshed. He faced the waterfall. 'Thanks Lord for sparing us.' There were many blessings for which to thank the Lord this morning, and he did so, going about a farmer's early chores, a burden in bad times and bad weather, a pleasure in good times and kindly weather such as now. The improvement in young livestock was a miracle.

Those tasks done, he took his invariable walk along the lake, and noticed a patch of oil making rainbows against the sun. Always something came to mar the moment that had seemed most perfect. How could he have known that there would be oil in the bowels of the machine? It was a small patch only, but could trout live with oil? That is just what they did with their inventions of the devil in times before, he thought. And there was that Eskimo boasting of his people's innocence in such matters. And here he came, and look what happened.

He was surprised to meet his neighbour so early at the

waterfall, but not pleased, for Smith wore a ferocious scowl, and growled: 'The woman said it was foolishness what we did.'

'My woman had the impertinence to say the same.'

'So I beat the woman, and she's been bawlin' half the night.'

'I have not yet punished mine, but shall. We did right, Neighbour. We should not pay heed to women's prattle.'

'Women and their blether. I'm telling you, Neighbour, we did right.'

Parker and Smith, sure of their rightness, yet ever mindful of incurring the Lord's displeasure, turned to salute the inscrutable Lord. As one man, they drew in gusty breath.

'Do you see what I see, Neighbour?'

'I see what you see, Neighbour.'

And what they saw they had seen but once before, eleven years ago, eleven notches on the giant sugar maple outside James Parker's cabin.

The Lord's pink ocean was not its uniform living pink. It was in turmoil, fingers of pink stabbing into blue, fingers of blue stabbing into pink, two armies locked in silent ever-changing ever-weaving battle. It was quite like those lights they sometimes saw in winter's night, lights of many colours that rippled and danced and probed and died across the northern sky. But these were of two colours only, pink and blue.

What was it that funny little fellow had said yesterday? *Our Lord in his infinite wisdom released the pink algae army to do battle with the filth and stink that wicked men down here poured into the waters of the Earth. And in due course, so leading scientists assure us, the war will be over, the oceans clean again, the task of the pink armies done. Then our Lord will suffer them to die. And then shall we, the Innuit, the people of our Lord, inherit the Earth.*

'Pink is winning, I fancy.'

'Ay. Yon funny wee chap said pink had to win many battles before the war would all be over.'

'But the Lord is revealing his pleasure with us. That will teach the women.'

'Ay, that'll learn them. No time to lose.'

James Parker jogged home at modest speed, no time to lose but energy to conserve. His woman and his child still slept. He shook Ruth awake.

'What is it?'

'A battle wages in the Lord's pink ocean.'

'Don't believe,' she muttered sleepily.

'Come out then, and see for yourself. Quick, woman!'

Ruth ran ahead of him up the valley to a first look-out point. The battle raged on, but the blues were undoubtedly in retreat. 'This is a nice soft mossy place. Come on, man, take me.'

James took her in quick, even brutal fashion, reminiscent of the beasts. 'My man!' she said, his happy slave. 'That is the best way for a woman. That was the best tumble we have ever had, and your seed is burning hot in me to make our baby. Now we are truly husband and wife.' And she took her left hand from his back and held it up to admire the copper ring which the Reverend Noel Avakana had provided yesterday.

Truly, women are foolish creatures, James Parker thought, falling for heathen marriage lines, rings on the fingers and all the rest.

'You promised to cherish me,' she said.

'You promised to obey me,' he said.

'So I always will, if you are your wise self again.'

They rested in that comfortable place, and then his woman roused him, wanting assurance made doubly sure, doubly slowly long and sure. 'Oh Lord,' she said and swooned away.

The morning was half spent when they awoke and stood to see that the Lord's pink ocean was entirely uniformly living pink. But the wind had swung from North to South, and on the fitful wind there came many scents to touch the nose, some faintly disgusting, some tangy in a prickling way.

'Those must be the stenches of which my mother often spoke.'

'Mine used to tell me that the stenches were quite horrible in Times Before. Ah, there is Mary.'

'We shall simply tell her that the funny little people flew away while she was sleeping. Got it?'

'Got it, James.'

'Mary!' And she waited there. Her eyes were black with thought. She would be wondering. 'I wanted to tell you, Mary, that those funny little people flew away while you were sleeping.'

'Did you, Daddy? Well, Ian's dad told him the same. But we said to one another that we couldn't have helped being woken up by the huge noise of that flying machine, and so we swum out to No-Man's-Island, and you're just a liar, Daddy, that's what you are.' Her lips were trembling. She was such a pretty hostile child of his.

'Mary!'

'Hush, woman. Why am I a liar, Mary?'

'Because of blood all over the grass where they were sleeping, and the scratches of the rocks you dragged, and the oil on the water where you sank their bodies in the flying machine. That's why, Daddy. You and Ian's dad, you murdered them. And perhaps Mummy did too.'

'I did not, Mary.'

'Mary,' James said. 'It caused us grievous pain to do this thing. It hurt us much more than it hurt those Eskimos, for we slew them mercifully with single strokes. But there were many reasons . . .' He tried to explain those many reasons to his small daughter who stared at him in horror. '. . . Perhaps you're too young to understand.'

'It's not me being too young to understand. It's you being too old to understand. You're always saying: '*Be kind, be nice and tell the truth*, and look at you. They were kind and nice and they told us the truth, and he said: *Thou shalt not kill*, and he said: *Love thy neighbour as thyself*, and he meant every word of it, he was a good laughing man even if he was crazy about that Jesus, and he explained things to Ian and me just as if we were grown-ups, which is more than you do, and so you killed him, and I hate you, I hate you, I hate you.' Mary sobbed desperately and ran away.

'She will get over it,' James said. 'Give the child comfort, woman.'

'I am your wife, and will not be given orders, *woman*, in that tone of voice, although I am a foolish woman, and I do not believe that Mary will get over it.'

'You wanted to do the same,' he called after her. 'Only in a less honest and less merciful way, and then you were disloyal to me.'

Ruth turned. She had a fine face, and a strong woman's body made for his. 'Perhaps I'm too old to understand,' she said, and followed young Mary.

'I was right,' James Parker said, alone beside the giant sugar maple which bore forty-five notches for himself, and forty-three notches for Ruth, his woman, and ten notches for Mary, their daughter. 'I was right. What else could I do?' But he was sorely troubled.

7

THAT moon grew old until it was a wan sliver in the morning sky. I've seen so many moons grow old, James thought. Each moon is born one evening there above the waterfall, and each moon dies one morning here above the waterfall. It is a mystery.

The moons were more of a mystery to him than the ocean, which remained uniformly pink. 'I haven't conceived,' Ruth told him, another mystery, another moon.

'In that case you're barren.' James Parker had not meant to speak the thought which had been growing in him for many months, but disappointment made him say harsh words.

'How can I be barren when the curse of the Lord is even now purging my womb? Might it not be, James, that your seed has lost its living spunk?'

That was an impertinence, although it was also a dark possibility that had crossed his mind. 'You were too late,' he said. 'You were so lazy that morning, remember, that the battle was over in the Lord's pink ocean before my seed could burn in you.'

'You're always perfect,' she said, spinning wool outside the cabin. That was a skill imparted to Ruth by her mother. 'James Parker is always the blameless one. It was even the poor Eskimo's fault that oil from his sunken flying machine polluted our water.'

Some trout had died, floating belly up, drifting slowly to the waterfall. But many had survived, and the oil was gone; and soon they would be spawning up the brook.

'There,' Ruth said. 'I think I have enough for Mary's little sweater thing. She has set her heart on it so much.'

James left his irritating woman, and went to tend his pleasing beasts. At the age of six months the young bull was already lusting, and must be penned alone. I will consult with Smith, James thought, as to when we should put the new blood to work. In that kind of thing, at least, he's been of some help to me, give the devil his due.

It was a confusing time for James. Quite often he thought that the day of the Eskimos had been a dream of his. He had so many dreams – such as of the wild geese flying, calling, alighting with mighty splashes on the lake. But he woke to darkness, to the puffing snores of Ruth, it was a dream of long ago.

That Eskimo had never come to feast on fatted lamb, to giggle and to preach about his dear Lord Jesus, to praise his own people, the Innuit, to join James and Ruth in heathen holy matrimony, to have a spin out over the Lord's pink ocean. And he, James Parker, had never tossed the medal honestly: *words up*, you do the funny little chap; *words down*, his woman. And he had never lost that toss and had never chopped Martha Avakana's head off with one merciful stroke in the light of the moon.

But then he would see the copper ring on Ruth's left hand, the upper garments called Mother Hubbards, those things that his womenfolk now insisted upon wearing at the least excuse. And he would see his good new axe-head, with the small man in the moon stamped on it, and James would know again that the day of the Eskimos was not a dream of his, but true in so far as any of life's dreams were true.

The oats were in, and the harvest moon was past its full rich size when clouds obscured it, and a warm moist wind blew up from the East, from the South, from points between. It was a fitful wind, now blustering around the cabin, now no wind at all.

'I don't like this wind,' James said. 'It may be the wild wind that has struck us a few times in my life at this season. Or it may not be. If the rain comes in a special fashion, we shall know.' His womenfolk listened to him in respectful silence.

The rain did come next morning in a special fashion. It was as if the Lord had upset a million buckets in the sky, and then the warm rain stopped as suddenly as it had begun, and the wild wind grew, and clouds raced low above the lake, and it was dusk in the middle of the morning hours.

As day wore on, the tempest uprooted many trees, snapped others off, and thundered at the Parkers' cabin; the rain was not now the upturning of one million buckets, but a million million buckets on and on. James told Ruth and Mary to sit on the side of the cabin away from the giant maple. But it was not the wind that he most feared for them all. It was the rain.

He went outside, fighting the door to close it behind him, then fighting the wind. Some gusts were strong enough to halt him in a wall of wind, some even drove him staggering back, but James struggled down to the shore of the lake, and along beside the fierce angry water. The rain lashed warmly at his bare head and body. He felt a sort of happiness in fighting the wild warm wind and rain until he reached the waterfall bridge and saw Smith at the other end of it. They did not venture onto the bridge, close beneath which a brown flood stormed. There was that known danger to fear and to avoid. But there might be a far worse danger, not to be avoided.

Surprisingly, Smith was the one who had first thought of it: *According to the old folk, your woman's dad said we were kept safe because the waterfall is broken by them ledges. But supposing there was ever such a muckle flood that the water skipped the ledges altogether. What then, Neighbour?* Smith spoke with the respect

of an unlettered man for the memory of Ruth's father, who
had been the prophet of the Lord.

The flood was still brown; the pink armies had not climbed;
and there was such a roaring that no man could tell what was
happening down the waterfall; and this was the worst flood
that James had seen. 'Spare us, Lord,' he said, hearing the same
words whipped from his neighbour.

James ran home with the wind and the rain at his back, and
perhaps they were abating now. 'All storms must pass,' he
said to himself, still afraid. 'All is well,' he said to his womenfolk who sat on the edge of the bed, their arms round one
another, and the wind was thundering. But suddenly the wind
died down, and suddenly the sun was shining, and soon the
wind blew mightily again, now from the West. 'It ends,' he
said. 'That's the sign.'

'James, you're brave.'

'Daddy, you're terrific,' Mary said, her first admiring words
since that time of the Eskimos.

The clearing of those windfalls, tangled together, lodged
high in other trees, his sorry oxen straining at the chain, made
much hard labour for James that winter.

But the forty-sixth year of his age was prosperous, and by
the forty-seventh, his beasts of mixed blood had reached
maturity. Then the old beasts could be slaughtered and pre-
served in the ice-house, tough meat, it was true, but plentiful.

'With my strong oxen,' James Parker said alone. The more
the women prattled on, the more silent he became in their
company, and the more he tended to talk with himself outside
in private. 'With my strong oxen, my warm new sheepskins,
my dozen eggs a day, my milk and cheese and butter, my fine
manure of every kind, I've become rich, or as rich as a plain-
ignorant farmer can be.' For all of which he thanked the Lord.

And he thanked the Lord also that his troublesome slipshod
neighbour had ceased to prey upon Parker reserves. 'I should

hope so,' James said, 'with that strong growing boy to help him.'

Mary also was growing fast, and was useful at everything but the heaviest work. She chattered often with her mother, women's talk about small things. But she had become a secret girl, never mentioning important matters to Ruth or to him, never speaking of that time of the Eskimos. Not even when they cocked anxious ears to some unfamiliar sound in the world beyond them would Mary speak of it, no reason to speak of it perhaps, for no flying machine had ever droned again.

So Mary was another mystery to him, a very sweet mystery, loving every bird and beast and bumble bee and flower. She would even smile, watching a mosquito on her hand as its body swelled with her good young blood until it flew sluggishly away. This love of every living thing might have come to Mary from her two grandfathers, those learned men. She would vanish whenever there was slaughtering to be done. But fortunately Mary ate meat with a growing girl's hearty appetite, another small mystery.

It was only when she played with Ian Smith that a different Mary showed herself. The laughter of the children was a lovely sound as they jousted with canoes out there, or raced their toboggans up there, or played in either junkpile, or swam together, the pale brown boy in his loincloth, the dark sleek girl in her two-piece suit of wool. That Eskimo and his woman must have long since rotted away at the bottom of the lake, but a certain prudery was their heirloom.

'Perhaps no bad thing, this prudery,' James said to himself. 'Even a man as ignorant as myself knows that there's a perfect innocence between those children together. There is indeed beauty to be seen in their companionship.' He caught the first broiler and chopped off its screeching head, and saved the blood for pudding. 'But they're both growing like mustard weeds. I must speak to Smith so that we can agree about the quickest and kindest way of ending their friendship in accordance with the Lord's commandments. We must separate them soon before nature dangles temptation to their innocence, yes, soon.'

'Very soon, James.' It was his woman come padding barefoot too quietly for his middle-aged ears, an annoying trick.

He caught the second broiler, chopped off its screeching head, and saved the blood for pudding. 'Come,' he said. 'You carry the bowl of blood. I'll carry the broilers, and even help you with the plucking. *Very soon*, you said. What very soon?'

'Very soon we must separate our Mary from that Smith boy. She's growing up.'

'I know that. Wasn't I saying it when you sneaked up on me?'

'And you were right, wise husband, but I have news for you. Mary *has* grown up. She has become a woman this very morning at the age of twelve.'

'Oh, Lord,' James said. 'So young.'

'Mary is no younger than I was when I became a woman. Or have you forgotten?'

'No,' James said. 'I haven't forgotten.' He had forgotten, but his mind took him back to long ago when he and Ruth were childhood cronies, and then one day he looked upon her with new tenderness, a miracle as innocent, and no sin. '. . . What were you saying?'

'Nature is nature, I was saying.'

'And beasts are beasts, and men are men.'

Ruth sighed. 'I know that. You needn't preach the Lord's commandments, which are as well known to me as they are to you, or better. It's only . . .' and she sighed again.

'It's only what?'

'It's only that they have been such good young friends together. Ian has cheered Mary from her moodiness. And look how she has improved his washing and his speech. But that's over. What must be, must be, and well I know it. James, could you take both broilers in your other hand, and hold my hand?'

And so they joined their hands, walking home from the henhouse. 'You have been my good woman these many years through storms and trouble.'

'And you my good man.'

'Dear wife,' he said. He used that word to please her. 'Don't cry, dear wife.'

'I'm crying for my blessings.'

'Where is Mary now?' he asked.

'She wanted to be alone, I think, and muttered more to herself than me about visiting some chipmunk in the old stone wall. This was a shock to her, and painful too.'

'But why a shock? Surely you had told Mary the facts of life?'

'Yes, but what is telling?' his woman said, her logic as ever a mystery. 'What is telling? And besides, hasn't she observed the facts of life in us all the years she can remember?'

'All the fruitless years,' James said.

'James, I've been thinking, and my thought is that we're ignorant people, not able to know whether I'm at fault, or you, or both of us. So wouldn't it be best that we should never mention that, nor even think of it?'

'That's a wise thought,' he said, and he kissed his woman on the cheek to show approval of her wisdom. 'From now on we shall simply love one another for the pleasure of true love.'

'But another thing's been in my mind, and especially this morning, and it is that the time has come for Mary to have her own private room, however small.'

'Yes,' James said. 'I thought of that, too. It would be proper now. Well, the seeds are sown, and the growing season not yet here, and I have some cedar logs. I can knock Mary up a little room in no time almost, if you both will help me.'

'Gladly,' Ruth said. 'And it will keep her mind off other things.'

Ruth scalded the broilers, and then plucked them outside the cabin. 'I'll race you,' he said.

She giggled, pleased with him for being boyish, and pleased because her nimble woman's fingers easily outplucked him, and that was that task done.

'I must speak to Robert Smith. For once we shall be in agreement, I'm quite sure.'

'And I'll speak to Janet Smith, who has grown fond of our Mary, just as I have grown fond of their Ian. But he's a white boy, and soon will be as coarse a white man as his father.'

'They may be rebellious at first. You know how wilful Mary can be. But we'll each arrange to keep them busy. Perhaps Smith might set him to build his own room, I will suggest that tactfully, anything to tide over a difficult time for the children. After all, they have been bosom friends.'

'Yes,' Ruth said. 'But there are bosoms and bosoms. Ah, here she comes.'

Mary did not come in the quiet pensiveness of mood that might befit a first meeting with womanhood. She came running, black-eyed, utterly distraught, what a beautiful angry child in tears on this morning of tears, holding something between her hands.

'Look!' she cried. 'Look Daddy and Mummy, look!' In her hands was a golden chipmunk, a tiny endearing black-striped beast, and it was dead.

'What happened?' James said. He knew, even if he did not quite understand, her love for every living thing.

'I was feeding Charlie Chipmunk, and he came with squeaks all the way from his home in the wall to fill his cheeks just bulging from my hand, and he ran back to store his crumbs, and he popped right out again to sit on a stone and think about me before coming for more, and there was a sort of thud, and poor Charlie Chip just flopped down dead, and that horrible disgusting beastly cruel bastard Ian Smith jumped out from some bushes with a war-whoop and that sling-shot he made from rubber in the Cadillac wreck, I told him it was ours not theirs but I let him have the rubber because he promised me faithfully he would never kill anything ever with it, and look what he did, the dirty Whitey, how I hate his stinking guts.'

8

FIRST, she found some rich topsoil and picked the pebbles from it. Next, she went to the old manure pile which had rotted down to crumbly blackness. Then she got some sand from the beach, and mixed them all together. It was lovely stuff for baby plants.

The tomatoes were still small, and not as sturdy as they should be, but that was Daddy's fault; he always sowed seeds too thickly.

Now she began to move the strongest of the seedlings from one box to the other. They would grow there until the moon had changed, and danger of a frost was over, and then her father would plant them out.

Of all Mary's family jobs she liked this one the best. You had to be so slow and thoughtful-handed. The tomatoes had a nice smell too. She did the same with lettuce, cauliflower and cabbage but the tender tomatoes were the most interesting. She kept them warm in her room at night.

While she worked, Mary hummed a tune, not thinking of it, the kind of tune that went on and on in your head and would not stop. Then she sang a bit:

> ' "My Bonny lies over the ocean,
> My Bonny lies over the sea,
> My Bonny lies over the ocean;
> Oh, bring back my Bonny to me." '

It was only when she had sung those words that she re-membered where the song had come from. But even then she could not escape the catchy tune, so she changed some words and sang again.

'You sing well, Mary,' said her father. 'I could hear as I came down from the brook, a sweet sound on the air. Would you sing again?'

' "My Lordy lies over pink ocean,
  My Lordy lies over pink sea . . ." '

'Mary!' he said sternly. 'How many times am I to tell you that the Lord is not for joking?'

'I was joking with the Lord, not at him.' Mary separated the tender roots, made a hole with her finger, and put it in and firmed it down. Grow well, she thought. 'Besides, I'm sure the Lord likes a laugh sometimes. You take the Lord so seriously, Daddy.'

'How could I take the Lord otherwise?' her father said. He was grey-headed now, and the skin of his arms and neck was no longer firm. He was a kindly man, but with a grudging temper; and if Mary still teased him sometimes, it was carefully.

'Daddy you sowed these much too thick. I wish you'd let me do it next year.'

'Gladly,' he said. 'My fingers were always clumsy thumbs, but now for close small things my eyes have become thumbs too.'

Mary laughed about his eyes being thumbs. He made nice small jokes like that, looking sad.

'What were you doing at the brook?'

'I went there because that Smith had opened the fence, and half his sheep were in our good top pasture from which I've even kept our own sheep until the grass is longer.'

'Why not make that Smith build a fence on his side where it ought to be?'

'I cannot *make* Smith do anything. There was a time some

years ago when he was better, almost helpful. Now I might as
well ask the man in the moon to build a fence. He simply
leered at me this morning, in the same leering way of that man
in the moon.'

'You're so funny, Daddy.'

'If I laugh, it's in order not to cry. It's because we must live
at peace, and that becomes harder. In the end he provoked me
into saying that a certain overgrown youth would be better
employed in building fences than in hunting rabbits with his
bow and arrow.'

'That boy just lives for killing things,' Mary said, shivered
at a memory, and planted the last tomato of the last row in the
box. Then she gave them all a real good soaking. 'Grow well,'
she said to the tomatoes.

'I was talking about my clumsy fingers being thumbs, but
your granny had another old saying. *To have a green thumb*, was
your granny's saying.'

'My thumbs are green from the tomatoes. Is that what
Granny's saying meant?'

'It meant that there's a magic in a green thumb that makes
all plants grow happily. And you have that magic, Mary, not
given to me, nor to your mother.'

'Not magic,' Mary said. 'It's just feeling you are them a
little bit. That isn't magic.'

'All love is magic, Mary.'

'Like you picking squabbles with Mummy, is that magic?'

Her father grunted, and he went away. I hurt his feelings,
Mary thought. He says such stupid soppy things that make me
want to, and they aren't what he's really like. She went by the
giant maple tree where there were fifty-one notches and forty-
nine notches for her old parents, and sixteen notches for herself. So it was six years, six times the wild pear had come into
blossom since that poor Eskimo had spoken of black people
far away up North, a few of them. Perhaps one will come in a

flying machine, Mary thought, a tall black prince, a strong black prince, a laughing wonderful black prince.

Now you're being stupid, she said to herself. She looked at the small garden she had made with rocks and earth, and to her rock garden she had brought the wildflowers of the valley, and some of the early ones were out – the starflowers in a shady place, red trilliums, the purple violets and the white. The names of these and many others had come down from her father's father who was a botanist in Times Before. *All love is magic*, Daddy said. Perhaps her green thumb was a magic, after all.

But Mary turned from her own wild garden to look down the valley, across the valley and up the valley, and everywhere at the edges of the fields the wild pear trees were coming out, a year's first blossom. The buds were touched with pink, but the open flowers were white, and in a few days snow-petals would fall dying into summer. He says I have a green thumb, she thought, but the loveliest flowers of all never felt my thumb. That is the Lord's green thumb, I can hear Daddy saying in his holy voice.

To Mary's father the Lord was all around everywhere in everything and all the time, the Lord's approval, the Lord's displeasure and the Lord's chastisement. But Mary wondered about what she hardly dared to think, being afraid of a Lord she doubted.

She went back to the cabin, and into her room, which had its own separate door. It had a window too, a cracked one from the remains of the trailer house which her grandparents had pulled with the Cadillac machine from that city called Boston just before the Lord's pink ocean. The main cabin had a bigger window taken from the Cadillac machine itself, the only one that had not been broken by bullets. Although her father had grunted and grumbled about taking those windows, he had taken them because a window was a window. But to him all the things in the junkpile, all the old inventions from Times Before were the things of men's madness that had incurred the Lord's increasing displeasure until in the end the Lord's patience was exhausted.

Mary laid out a fresh sheet of birchbark, her new quill pen, and she made soot-ink. But her poem to the wild pear or the shadbush or the saskatoon, coming so softly, dying so soon – it would not seem to come. She tried very hard, but it would not come. 'Won't come,' she said. 'Green thumb,' feeling sleepy and stupid, so she lay down, and sleep after gardening in the morning was lovelier than any wild pear tree.

'Mary! Where is that girl?'

I'm not *that* girl, Mary thought. I'm me.

'She was pricking out tomatoes when last I saw her. At least that's one thing she enjoys and does so well – her gardening. But . . .'

'But what, James? Must you always stop at *but*?'

'Can you never give me time to express my thoughts? But she is very changeable in mood – one moment sunny, the next downright rude.'

'She's at a difficult age, half child, half woman. Can't you understand this?'

'But she is sixteen years old, and fully grown, that's obvious.'

'In her splendid curving body, that's obvious, but in her mind? A girl's mind is full of dreams. Besides, James, you annoy her with old-fashioned prosiness.'

'Is it old-fashioned prosiness to rebuke her when she mocks the Lord?'

'That depends on the rebuke. And Mary doesn't mean to mock the Lord. She means to mock your holiest holy look whenever the Lord's name is mentioned. She told me yesterday that she is sure the Lord has a darned good laugh at you about it.'

'So you've been conspiring against me with our daughter.'

'I don't understand you, James. I try my best to be a loving wife, but you have become a stranger to me, so pompous and so quarrelsome.'

Mary went in. 'Squabbling again,' she said. 'And I'm not worth squabbling about, so you're being stupid.'

'Yes, we are stupid,' her father said.

'You are all that we have, dear Mary,' said her mother. 'Hence our stupid squabbles.'

'It's my fault for being bitchy,' Mary said. 'Gosh, I'm hungry.' It was rabbit stew for dinner.

Mary made the small chirping noises of the chipmunk; and in a while it answered from inside the wall. Daddy said that the wall might have been there since the very beginning of Times Before, when settler people first came to this valley, making fields from the forest, picking rocks and stones from the fields, piling them into untidy walls.

'Come on, Charlie Chip,' she said. 'Come out!'

He showed his head along the wall for one quick look, and disappeared. But the next time he was much closer. 'I won't hurt you,' she said. 'Eat your nice oatmeal up.' She had made a pile of it between her and the wall.

But this chipmunk was a stranger, the first one who had come to live here since that other one. 'I'm going to be your friend,' Mary said. 'Come on!' She talked to him, or it might be to her, until the chipmunk seemed to know that this was a friendly giant, and it popped out to fill its cheeks with oatmeal and scurried back to store that.

Then she wondered if it was right to make the chipmunk tame, because he might become careless and forget about the weasels that lived in stone walls too. But perhaps there was no escape for Charlie Chipmunk if the slim deadly weasel decided to hunt him down.

'See you later,' Mary said, 'I hope,' her mind full of the dangers in this valley which was safe for her.

She had spoken to Ian Smith only once in the four years since that other time. It was up near the head of the valley beside the brook. She had been sitting, and the noise of the water had prevented her hearing movement, but there he suddenly was on the other side, bow in his hand, arrows in a quiver.

What are you killing now? More chipmunks for fun?

He had gone quite pale at the sight of her. *I'm hunting rabbits*, he said. *Besides, how was I to know you had a pet chipmunk?*

You did it for horrible cruel fun, though. Well, didn't you? Not even to eat.

I'm hunting rabbits to eat, he said. *There are too many of them because they haven't enough enemies, Dad says.*

Which was true, and her own father said the same and he hunted their rabbits, and she ate them too, and they were good. *It's still for fun*, Mary said. *And if you ever kill anything on our land like you did the last time, I'll kill you.*

I believe you would, you daft wee bitch, he said, and went away.

Daft wee bitch, she hated him more, remembering it.

Since that time last fall, Mary hardly ever went to the head of the valley because it narrowed to the springs, and if Ian Smith came up, she would be trapped. But she had seen him after dinner today across the lake, going down to the waterfall. So it was safe to climb this afternoon, picking violets, the purple ones. They were pretty in her yellow sweater. She had dyed the wool herself with crushed dandelions boiled in a mixture of water and sheep dung. The colour was lovely even if it did come off a little when the wool was wet. I must watch out for rain, she thought. Dark clouds sailed, and sunshine came and went.

From the spring, Mary looked down the way she had come, over the woods and at the blue lake where the shadows of those clouds were sailing, and at the pale blossoms along the fields, and out, far out, to the ocean glowing.

Her father and mother seemed almost to worship the Lord's pink ocean, believing that old story about one day it would die, and the ocean would be blue again. But Mary hated it, not even knowing for sure that the pink ocean and the pink waterland were dangerous, keeping them prisoners out of fear. *You must never go Outside, Mary. Never, never, never. Do you promise?*

Again and again and again, the very first words she could remember. And she had never been Outside, although when she was small she used to go right up to the barricade in the West Ravine to see a woodchuck. But no woodchucks lived there any more. Perhaps the woodchucks had strayed Outside. It would not be difficult, it would be much too easy for a small animal to find its way through that barricade and the ravine.

But here you had to scramble up steeply, holding on to roots and rocks if you wanted to see over to the dead hills and valleys that stretched all the hundreds or thousands or was it millions of miles to the cold land of the Eskimos where other people lived, and nobody between, that Eskimo had said.

'I don't believe it,' Mary said. 'If there are other blue lakes, there must be other blue people.' She laughed at her private joke, and climbed. It was quite safe to look over. Daddy often did.

The rock sloped smoothly a short distance down to the North, about steep enough for a toboggan run. It was quite bare of earth except where one wide crack ran across the rock. In the next valley the pink river flowed, and pink streams into that, so it looked like a fish's backbone, pink. In flatter places, a few grey dead trees still stood. There was no green at all. It was grey and dead, or it was pink and alive. Her father said that the hillsides were down to bare rock because there were no living roots to hold the stones and earth that they heard rumble down the dead hills beyond, but not so often nowadays because most of them had slid already to make great untidy piles at the foot of each hill, and to make pink ponds and bogs.

But the first slopes were not messy or horrible. They were washed quite clean almost everywhere by all the rains of all the years. The bare rocks were safe enough, or Ian Smith would not have picked up that medal thing on the other side above the Smiths' cabin. That medal had told them something about trading the farm animals, she could not quite remember.

'It's always remembering or not remembering,' Mary said as she climbed down again. 'It's always stupid old things before. Nothing ever new, nothing ever coming. Oh well, there are the plants, and friends to make with new Charlie Chipmunk. It's just old unhappy people, and me alone, and no black prince.' She saw him suddenly, stepping down to the float of the flying machine, and coiling a rope and laughing, and calling in a deep strong voice: *Catch, Mary*! The sun had gone in, and now she felt a drop of rain, but Mary sat on with many thoughts.

She heard a scream. It was the high scream that a rabbit made when the killing weasel took its throat.

The rabbit came, not screaming any more, but fleeing. It fled desperately uphill and past her, still splodged with the white of its winter coat. Its long back legs were not working well because in its hindquarters was an arrow that flipped and flopped and swayed about. It was heading straight for the place where Mary herself had just scrambled up to see Outside.

'Stop, Rabbit!' she cried, but that only made the rabbit

struggle more desperately, and she chased it. Wounded, with the arrow stuck deeply in, it would never be able to climb the steep slope, and she could catch it, she almost caught it.

The rabbit scrabbled on three legs, slipped back, screamed again, and was over, gone Outside.

9

MARY lay there. Her hand had even touched the soft fur of the rabbit, poor screaming rabbit, gone. She climbed on, and the rain began. It rained heavily, but the sun was shining on dead lands to the North.

The rain made dancing splashes on the bare rock below her. The rabbit crouched now at the foot of the slope which ended at a precipice. It strained round to tug at the arrow with its rabbit teeth, but the arrow would not come.

Was the rock safe? Pink did not climb bare rock, Daddy said. *Dare I*? Mary thought, and the rabbit screamed. 'I'm coming, Rabbit,' she called. 'Don't worry, Rabbit, I'm coming down.' She knew that a quiet voice could soothe any frightened animal if she went on talking long enough, like a skunk that got its head stuck in a can on the junkpile, and she had talked and talked until it had let her take the can off without even spraying her. 'It's all right, Rabbit,' she called. 'I'm coming.' And she went on, talking all the time in that special voice.

There was one wide crack across the rock, about as wide as Mary was tall, and in it was grey earth. She jumped across that to rock again, her bare feet on the smooth wet rock. It was not slippery.

'Come back, Mary! Quick! Come back!'

His arrow flipped and flopped in the rabbit's back. 'It's all right, Rabbit,' she said, close now. 'Good rabbit, it's only me.'

She had not had long enough to soothe the rabbit, or the pain was too bad for it to hear her, because the rabbit ran away again. It ran across above the precipice to where that ended.

But the rock over there was not bare, nor was the wet earth grey. It was pink.

'Stop, Rabbit!' she shouted. The rabbit's front paws touched pink earth, and its last scream stopped short as it jumped, three stiff legs and one leg dangling, its body arched. Then the rabbit lay still.

Mary saw the pink climbing through wet grey earth. It climbed fast up the side of the bare slope down which she had just come. It bubbled and heaved, alive. It was hunting, and she knew what it would do. It would cross the wide crack above her. She looked over to the right and saw it coming the other way. The pink armies were meeting like pincers. They had met, and she could not move.

But here was Ian Smith. He took her by the shoulder of her yellow sweater, and he shook her. 'Jump it!' he said. 'Jump it, lassie!' He shook her harder, but she could not move.

He pulled her with him to the crack, and then he picked her up and threw her over the pink living beast. She fell on the other side, and he jumped to drag her from the pink that surged at them on bare rock, fell back, surged, fell back. Then they were safe.

The rain had stopped, and two rainbows, a bright one, a dim one, curved across dark clouds. One end of the brighter rainbow met the earth in their own green valley, the other in dead hills beyond. 'Where my folk came from once upon a time,' said Ian Smith, 'there was a saying that you would find treasure where the rainbow ended. Did I hurt you, Mary?'

She shook her head. 'Bruises,' she said. But she could not stop crying. She cried and cried for all the things.

After a while she was crying less; and then she had stopped crying.

'It's bonny,' he said, looking down at their valley, fresh from a spring shower of rain, and so it was. The rainbows had gone.

'Did you see your arrow flipping and flopping, and the rabbit trying to pull it out?'

'Yes,' he said.

'That wasn't so bonny. And the dead pink rabbit wasn't so bonny.'

'No,' he said. He stood, went over to his bow which lay beside the spring, picked it up and spun it away downhill.

'What did you do that for?'

'Because I made a bad shot, and I nearly killed you.'

'Well, you saved me too. I could have been pink and dead, not black.'

Ian laughed. 'You're comical,' he said.

She gave a long shudder after crying. 'I don't feel comical. I never saw the pink kill anything before.'

'Nor did I.'

'I didn't quite believe it would.'

'Well, I did, but I always sort of wondered too if they made it up just to keep us in.'

'Same here. The Eskimos told us, though.'

'Yeah, and they chopped those Eskimos pretty quick.'

'And the pink killed quickly, not like your arrow.'

'Can't you stop it about my arrow?'

'Why should I? It was for fun, and it was cruel.'

'It was hunting,' he said. 'I was hunting for meat. Don't you eat meat?'

'Yes,' Mary said. She had eaten rabbit not long ago. 'But I was remembering the chipmunk. Always remembering, that's the trouble. Nothing ever new, and us alive in a huge dead world with silly old people bearing grudges, and nothing ever new or different. Do you know what I mean?'

Ian looked at her. His face was not young and cruel. It was young and kind. 'You're sort of new and different,' he said.

Mary stood. Her hip was sore from falling on the rock over there Outside. 'Let's go and find your bow,' she said.

The string of the bow had caught on an alder by the brook. 'From now on I'll shoot for the head,' Ian said. 'Kill or miss, and no barbs in the arrows, that isn't cruel.'

'No,' she said. 'That isn't cruel, I suppose.'

'I hear something. Quick!'

They hid in bushes on the Parker side. It was Robert Smith, grey-headed, white-bearded, and he was scowling. He looked at the ground, uphill, across the brook, and his eyes came to them, went past them. He turned a full circle to scowl at the ground. 'Och, fuck it!' he said, and spat, and went downhill through his evergreen woods.

'Did he see us?'

'Don't be daft. If he'd seen us . . . ' But Ian did not finish.

'Why the *Och, fuck it*! and the spit?'

'Mebbe he saw my tracks. I crossed the burn there after the rabbit. But that's what Dad's like, always angry at something, picking fights with Mum, and nothing I do is ever right.'

'Mine keeps talking about having to live in peace or not live at all, but he *wants* to hate your dad. Still, it wasn't fair to pull down our fence this morning.'

'That's Dad's idea of a joke. Well, the next time he beats Mum, I'll show the old bastard something.'

'Are you strong enough?' But her sore hip reminded Mary of Ian's strength.

He did not answer. 'It isn't as if we're hungry any more. The beasts are strong, and we've lots of everything.'

'That could be it. Perhaps people get like that when they have enough.'

'We don't know any other people to know by,' Ian said. 'Or it could be because they murdered those Eskimos, so they blame one another. Or it could be living all their lives with the Lord's pink ocean, hoping and hoping, and it never changes, and now they're old. I expect it's pretty well everything.'

'I think it's: *They're not our kind of people too*. He's been saying that for ever, and Mummy used to, but she says it less. *They're not our kind of people* because you're white and we're black.'

'You're not even black,' Ian said. 'You're brown like some old oak leaf.'

'You're not even white,' Mary said. 'You're pink like the Lord's pink ocean except when you're going as red as a beet-root from laughing.'

She led the way down the Parker path beside the brook. 'Would you like to meet my new Charlie Chipmunk? He isn't tame yet, not properly.'

'I'd like that fine,' Ian said, behind her.

He had a man's voice now, but he seemed the same easy friend he had been before, before he killed that other chipmunk, before she had hated him, before they grew up.

'It's all crazy,' Mary said. 'And I'm the craziest. I never thought you'd be the same.'

'Nor did I you,' he said. 'Hang on a mo'. I'll have a look round.' He stretched for the lowest limb of a tall spruce on Smith land, just across the brook, swung a leg over and climbed quickly out of sight. 'All clear,' he called down. 'The four of them are twos and twos among the vegetables.'

'I can't even see you miles up there,' Mary said.

'Want to look at something? Here it comes.'

The something came down on the end of an electric cable. It was a kind of double wheel, quite wide, with crooked slates. 'What is it?' she asked.

'I'll explain.' The wheel went up, and soon Ian came down. 'Remember that spinner on the flying machine?'

Mary nodded.

'Well, it pulled the machine along because the spinner pushed back the air. So I got thinking. If the spinner could do it to the air, why couldn't water flowing in the burn do the same thing to the wheel? See what I mean?'

'Well, sort of,' Mary said. 'But water can't climb a tree.'

Ian laughed. 'You're daft,' he said.

'Daftie yourself. Go on.'

'I keep it up there because I have to hide it from my father. He thinks anything new like an experiment is against the Lord's commandments. He hates machines.'

'So does mine. He thinks they caused the madness in Times Before. Daddy thinks mad men made machines, or men made mad machines, or something.'

'Even when I wanted to fix the old hay mower on our junk-pile he got in a rage. So I built my tree house where I can work on new inventions.'

'A house? I can't see anything.'

'It's hidden with branches. But I can watch the whole valley from there, and if I know where five people are, I know I'm safe, even making some noise.'

'You're safe now if I don't tell on you.'

'I wouldn't if I was you,' he said, not friendly at all.

'Well, don't say you're safe from *me*, then. Of course I won't tell on you. Can I climb up to the house?'

'One of these fine days, you can.'

'Why not now?'

'Because it's my house and it's in a mess, and because I say so.'

'You don't have to be bossy,' Mary said. 'I just wondered what it's like. Does it keep the rain out?'

'That's a pretty stupid question. If it didn't, things would get all rusted up again.'

'Well, I'm not an inventor. I don't even see what that wheel is for.'

'If the water turns the wheel, and the wheel turns a shaft, and the shaft turns something else, that's what it's for.'

'But what's the something else?'

'A stone for sharpening, a mill for grinding grain, and so on. Other things,' he said vaguely.

'You're holding out on me. But what's the use of new inventions if he won't even let you put your wheel in the water?'

Ian looked at her. 'My dad isn't going to live for ever.'

'No,' she said. 'I wish Mummy could, though.'

They walked down. 'So do I. Mum's fun when she isn't scared of him. But what I wish most is that another flying machine would come.'

'I think that all the time.' And again Mary saw her black prince stepping from the flying machine.

'We wouldn't let those old bastards kill the next ones.'

'No, we wouldn't,' Mary said. The sun had moved round to suppertime. 'I'll have to go home, but come and see Charlie Chipmunk.' She took some damp oatmeal from her skirt pocket, put it on the stone and called the chipmunk. Its head came out, but not the rest of it. 'He doesn't trust you,' Mary said. 'And I don't wonder. Go back a bit.'

Ian smiled. 'You were aye a sharp-tongued wee bezzom,' he said in the broad speech he had used when first they were friends.

He went back a bit, and the chipmunk came out to fill its cheeks and return to store. The next time it took the oats from Mary's hand.

'That's a kind sight to see,' Ian said, and the chipmunk fled. 'I'm sorry for killing the other one. I didn't just think in those days much.'

'It's the nature of boys, Mummy told me then. But that's long ago and now we're friends again and thanks for saving me, Ian.'

'Och, away!' he said. 'I was thinking . . . I was thinking . . .'

'Are you sure? Well, what?'

He ignored her small old joke about him thinking. Ian

Smith would seem so slow in his thinking, and then you would find that he had been thinking ahead of you all the time.

Mary put out the rest of her oatmeal for the chipmunk. 'Look at my wrists, all yellow from the sweater. That's an invention you could make – something to stop the colour coming off when it gets wet.'

But he paid no attention about her new yellow sweater. He frowned. 'I wonder,' he said. 'I was thinking that there's a few things from the Cadillac machine I could use in an invention.'

'Oh, Gosh!' Mary said. 'We'd have to be careful. Daddy's death on touching anything from it.'

'Well,' Ian said. 'If you just happened to be walking up your side of the burn after supper tomorrow, and you just happened to give a wee whistle, and I just happened to call down that the coast was clear, and you just happened to climb up to see my tree house, I just might happen to explain what it is I'm after.'

'Just might,' Mary said. 'Cheerio, then.'

'Cheerio,' he said.

Mary ran home, late for supper.

10

'MARY, only yesterday I praised your green thumb. Yet only last night you forgot to take in the tender plants.'

'So I forgot. So what? Well, I didn't forget, Daddy, and it didn't freeze. My green thumb told me.' But she had forgotten.

'Mary, you mustn't be so rude . . . Mary, however did you get that awful bruise? . . . And, Mary, look at your lovely new sweater, ruined.'

'I was caught in the rain, and it isn't ruined, just a bit streaky. I slipped and fell at the old stone wall, that's how I got a bruise. Any other questions?'

'Mary, what were you doing at the old stone wall?'

'Really, James, she has a perfect right . . .'

'Silence, woman! Answer me, Mary!'

'I was taming my new chipmunk friend, if you want to know.'

'Is it wise or even fair to tame a new chipmunk friend when you know what that Smith boy will do to it?'

'That Smith boy knows what I'll do to him if he does it to it.'

'How does he know that, Mary?'

'Because I saw him across the brook last year, and I shouted at him, that's how.'

'Did you have your new chipmunk friend last year?'

'No, Daddy, I did not. I told him if he ever killed *anything* on our land again, I'd kill him.'

'Quite right, Mary, I approve.'

'James, how can you approve such a . . . ?'

Mary escaped them and their new squabble. But she worked hard all afternoon sowing corn and then helping a cow to calve, pleasing her father so much that he asked no more suspicious questions and was told no lies.

After supper he had his usual snooze, and she told her mother that she was going to collect dogtooth violets for her garden. 'You have such energy, dear.'

Mary whistled, and he called back from the heights: 'You'll have to jump for the first branch.'

It took her several jumps before she got both hands over, swing, arms bend, knee on and up. Her hip was sore. 'That's fine,' Ian said, but she could not see him high up there. 'Now it's easier than a ladder. Just don't look down.'

Mary climbed, and it certainly was easy, but a longer and longer way to fall. She stopped for a rest. 'Look up now.'

She looked up to see green spruce needles, and then to make out through them the floor of the tree house. It was not built against the trunk, but away from it, and the last climb was on a wooden ladder to a door where Ian knelt. 'Even if you fell, you'd only loop yourself around a branch or two. Come on!'

'Oh, Lord,' she said. 'It's miles down there.'

'Don't look, I told you. Come on!'

Mary was scared of that ladder, sloping out from the trunk, but she managed it, and his hand caught hers and she was safely in. The tree house was big enough to stand and to move around a little, almost as big as Mary's room at home. But there was nothing on the floor except Ian's wheel and some tools and strange old machineries. 'Oh, Gosh!' she said. 'How did you manage to build it up here – I mean even the noise of hammering?'

'I didn't,' he said. 'I told him I was making us a toolshed from the boards in the old barn, and so I made us two instead of one, and I nailed the walls and floor and roof of this house each separately. Then I brought the floor first, and once I had that hoisted up and anchored good and solid with electric wire, well, the rest was easy except for a few near squeaks from Dad. Well, not so easy, it took me a whole year to make it.'

'I should think so,' Mary said. 'What a super house.' She went to look through the window, and Ian went back to whatever he was doing with that wheel.

It was a wooden window with hinges at the top, held open by a wire from the ceiling. She had looked for the tree house on the way from home, knowing that it was in the tallest spruce, but could see nothing. From here, though, looking out through green branch-tips swaying near her in the breeze, she had a perfect view of the lake and valley, all of it – the two cabins smoking, the beasts, the fields, the wild pear white as snow. It was calm down at the lake, and trout made circles, feeding. 'I feel like king of everything,' Mary said.

'Queen,' he said. 'King Charles the First, they chopped his head off. And Mary Queen of Scots, they chopped hers too. My mum knows all those dirty old English choppings off by heart. Come on you, fit! You're Mary too,' he said. 'You'd better watch you don't get chopped. Ah, that's better.'

It was hard to tell which he was talking to, the wheel or her. Now she looked beyond their valley, and she sang it:

> ' "My Lordy lies over pink ocean,
>   My Lordy lies over pink sea,
>   My Lordy lies over pink ocean,
>   Oh, bring back my Lordy to me." '

'You're a caution,' Ian said.
'How do you mean, a caution?'
'That's Scotch for funny.'

But Mary was thinking of yesterday. 'That pink wasn't such a caution.'

'No,' he said.

Mary left the window and sat on the floor to watch him work. He was fitting the metal rod – a shaft he had called it – to the centre of the wheel. His hands were big, but his fingers felt here, felt there, fingers thinking for him. Like my green thumb thinks with plants, Mary thought. And she thought: I wish Daddy was like he used to be when I was small.

Ian laid it down and looked at it. 'Dad did see my footmarks yesterday, and blood too.'

'What did you say?'

'I said I didn't dare cross the brook, and he only grunted, it was easy. I should have said you and me took a wee stroll Outside together. That would have made the old man sit up. He's never been Outside himself.'

'Nor has mine. But we both have.'

'Me one more time than you,' Ian said, pleased with himself. He was a bit cocky and pleased with himself. 'Did yours ask any awkward questions?'

'They sure did, and all the lies I had to tell. Lies are like snowballs. I told whoppers until I was tied up in knots but they swallowed them, even about bruising myself on that stone wall.'

'All you said to me was *bruises*. What bruises?'

'Just on my hip,' she said, feeling her face get hot.

'Oh, I see,' Ian said, looking at his invention. 'Well, that's the best I can do. Now, about the Cadillac machine . . .'

'What about it?'

'It made its own electric is what about it. I remembered the insides from when we used to play there, so I snuk over lately, and now I've got it figured out – how and what did it and the wires and everything.'

'You think you're clever, don't you?'

'Not specially,' Ian said. 'It isn't like starting out from nothing. It's all there to see how it worked in Times Before. So you just have to look and think and look and think until you get the idea of it. If I could make that thing turn quick enough, and fix two wires to one of those glass eyes in front for lights, at night, they must have been, then we could have the electric, see?'

'Oh, Gosh!' Mary said. 'Gosh, yes, I see. But wouldn't Daddy be sure to notice? How big is it?'

'About the size of a birch log for the stove, not big. My dad never missed all these tools and things, so why would yours? Besides, the nose of the Cadillac machine is always closed, so how would he notice?'

'Would it take long to get?'

'That depends on the nuts that hold it. I oiled them, but you can't tell until you use a wrench. If they're rusted solid, then it's hopeless. Well, when do we try?'

'You've forgotten something. It's our Cadillac machine, not yours. You haven't even asked me yet.'

'That's stupid,' Ian said. 'I can't do it unless you'll be sentry. So I'm asking, amn't I?'

'You could ask me more nicely,' Mary said. 'Well, okay. But what time is best? Mummy stays in, and Daddy snoozes after supper.' She stood and looked out of the window. Nobody moved down there. 'We'll have to be terribly careful, Ian. If Daddy caught you, or worse still – if he found out I was being sentry . . . Well, I mean he could do just anything.'

'I know,' Ian said, and then he said in his broad speech: 'Dinna fash yerself, wee lassie. That means: Don't worry, baby girl.'

'I wish you wouldn't talk that awful Scotch. And don't call me baby girl.'

'You're a good sport whatever size you are, and that's big enough.'

'Well, thanks.'

'I've simply got to have that thing. If it failed, then there would only be my steam machine, more difficult, less interesting.'

'What's your steam machine?'

'The lid of the hot pot goes hoppety-hop. You've seen it, eh?'

'Yeah, sure.'

'Well, it started my thinking in that direction.'

'Oh, Lord!' she said. 'There's Daddy, and he's started his walking in this direction. I'll have to fly.'

'Climb down would be better,' Ian said, still fiddling. But he looked up. 'You're great,' he said. 'Same time tomorrow. Give us a whistle. Cheerio, then.' And he went on with his invention.

'You've got that electric on the brain. Cheerio.'

Going down was not very nice because she had to look down, but the height did get less. Mary dropped from the lowest limb, jumped fast water below the pool and was safe on Parker land.

Dogtooth violets had been her reason or excuse, and there were lots of them in the hardwood forest. Mary strolled that way, expecting to meet her father, but she heard his voice before he came into view, talking to himself again, and what he was saying made Mary plunge beneath a bushy cedar.

'. . . Her eyes were glittering, all her life a sign of mischief – that, and the petulance. What a worry that child is to me. And Ruth – nag nag nag from morning to night until I'm an interloper in my own home with one fat old woman and one bad-tempered daughter. Forgive me, Lord, for speaking my most private thoughts. But if you could see your way soon to win the pink ocean war, then a buxom bird might step from a flying machine into my arms. I don't mean some silly little virgin thing, but one amply skilled in rough and tumble. Is this too much for a hen-pecked chap to ask? I mean no familiarity, Lord . . .'

James Parker's deep voice faded away uphill, and Mary came out. 'The dirty old man,' she said. 'Now sex on top of everything. Just think of it at fifty-one. My daddy surely has gone crazy.'

The dogtooth violets had finished flowering, but their mottled leaves made them easy to find. She wrapped the bulby roots in moss. Dogtooth violets were not violets, and the wild pear was not a pear, and Ian was not an inventor, and Daddy was not dreaming about some fat black female stepping from some flying machine.

'What's the joke, dear?' her mother said.

'Oh, just everything.'

'It's lovely to hear that laugh of yours again.'

The place Mary had chosen for sentry duty was the least suspicious one, her chickadee place at the crabapple tree where she left crumbs for them every day and kept suet hanging from a wire. Now she sat against the trunk, the piece of suet in her hand, and that rested on her knee. My knee is a nice brown colour, Mary thought. Like some old oak leaf. She could not whistle for the chickadees this evening, because that was to be the warning signal to Ian behind her over the rise at the West Ravine. Nothing stirred down at the cabin.

She heard some squeaks, and that might mean that he was managing to turn the nuts which held the electric-maker to the whole machine. Mary turned her head and called him. He was not far away.

'Yeah?'

'You're taking simply ages.'

'Nearly done.' He was out of sight of her, and out of sight from the cabin. But there was a high open ridge, in full view of anyone from anywhere, and he would have to cross that to reach the Parker woods.

Now chickadees arrived to make busy-beezings in the tree above her, wanting suet. Then one was on her finger, pecking at delicious fat. 'Hi, bold chickadee,' she said. 'Your head is as black as mine, and your beady eyes are blacker, much.' Then another came to take its place, so light a bird that she could not even feel its weight, but the claws were strong around her finger. It was nice about them the way each took its turn.

'Any more of you up there?' Mary said, and looked to see.

Beyond the apple-buds and beyond the friendly chickadees, far beyond in the deep blue of the sky, a white thing moved or made itself. It was like a white needle pushing into nothing. It was nothing or it was something. Was that a tiny glint of sunlight at the needle's point?

'Look at the sky, Ian!' Mary called; then remembered being sentry and turned to the cabin, but nobody stirred. She heard no sound, not the smallest whisper, but something had climbed the sky from the North, and something was going down the hill of the sky to the South. The white needle broadened to a pencil, and the white pencil broadened to a tail of cloud, now wide and fuzzy where it came from, sharp needle where it went, dipping down to meet the Lord's pink ocean, gone. But the white ribbon of cloud still spread in ripples, like those clouds that told of wind to come. In the North the cloud had widened to feathery wisps, to nothing.

Mary heard the door of the cabin open, and got ready to whistle if either of them should come this way. It was her father. He looked down the lake to the waterfall, the first thing he always did; but then he must have noticed the white cloud, because his head went up and he turned this way to follow it back. There was a loud click over the hill, Ian shutting down the nose of the Cadillac machine, and Daddy had heard that, he was coming. Mary gave her warning whistle, the high note and two low notes of the chickadee, but louder. He was walking quickly.

'Oh, Daddy, you've frightened away my chickadees, that's mean.'

'I heard a sound from the West Ravine. What was that sound?'

'I didn't hear any sound, and if I didn't, how could you, as deaf as some post?'

That made it worse. He glared suspiciously at her.

'Do you see that strange cloud, Daddy?' By this time the cloud had drifted into woolly white squiggles across the sky, not so strange.

'That's the cloud of tomorrow's wind,' he said, dismissing her and it. 'Now I shall investigate.' He strode on.

Ian was trapped. He could not escape unseen across the open land. He could not climb through the terrible tangle of the barricade in the West Ravine to hide Outside where the bogs were pink. There was nowhere in the Cadillac machine or under it.

I'll scream and scream and have a fit and twist about in agony, Mary thought. There was no other hope. Then the miracle happened. First there had been the miracle of the white needle in the sky. Now there was this other miracle, which once had come from the sky.

On the surface of the lake, unbroken until now except by feeding trout, something was floating. Below No-Man's-Island at the bottomless place a long flat thing floated. It was dirty from being down there so long, but still mustardy-coloured. It was a wing of the flying machine.

'Look, Daddy!' Mary shrieked. 'Just look!'

Her father turned at her wild cry.

'Oh, Lord!' he said. 'Oh, Great Jehovah. That invention of the devil!'

He ran past her. He surely could run for an old chap of fifty-one, past the cabin and to the shore. The canoe shot out in a paddle-flurry. Soon another canoe was racing across the lake. Ian's dad and Mary's daddy converged on the wing of that flying machine.

'Okay, Ian,' Mary called. 'It's safe now. See you later.'

11

'WHAT are they doing?'

'Still arguing. But I can't hear the shouting match exactly. I think yours wants to burn it on a bonfire, and mine wants to sink it where it came from.'

'Yours is right. It's made of metal, and any old dope except Dad knows that won't burn.'

'Now they've left it. They're both paddling home in a terrific hurry. Ian!'

'Well, what is it?'

'Couldn't you leave that thing for just a single minute and talk about what we saw in the sky?'

'Now, this fits in there, and that goes on this way. I have to remember each single piece.' Ian laid down the wrench and looked at her, his eyes vague with thinking about that beloved electric-maker, which he had started already to take to bits. But he gave his head a shake. 'Okay, shoot!'

'Daddy said they used to ride rockets in Times Before, like when they went for picnics to the moon. Could it have been a rocket?'

'Dunno. Dunno what a rocket is or was. Besides, there isn't any moon just now.'

'You're not much help. Well, could it have been a flying machine miles and miles up there too far away to hear? Ian, concentrate!'

Ian stood and came over to the window. ' I couldn't look at it for long, but I did think I saw a shiny speck in front, like a silvery arrowhead quite like.'

'So did I.'

'And it was going South. What was it that Eskimo said?'

'He said there were scientist chaps far away down South in the Antarctic. So it could be some mercy mission.'

'Or it could be them bearing the word of their dear Lord Jesus.'

'Gosh, Ian, you're a caution.'

'Thanks. All the same, I did quite like the sound of that Jesus guy, what I can remember.'

'Yeah, sort of decent.'

'Here's something: Did that wing pop up before, or during, or after it had gone? I mean, if it was some flying machine, and they saw the wing, it could be not too good for our reputation.'

'You're right. But it was after. I know because I saw it pop up like some miracle just when I was desperate to stop him.'

'Well, back to work. This job is going to take a long time – an hour is all I dare each evening, or he's sure to be suspicious. But if I get it working, that'll be a different story.'

'How, a different story?'

'Because I can do night-shifts, stupid, on more inventions.'

'Oh, I see. There they go again.' Two canoes fairly skimmed across the lake, and soon two fathers chopped with axes, clang, hollow clang along the wing to meet. 'Oh, Lord!' Mary said.

'What is it?' Ian came to look. The two men had stopped chopping, and were shaking axes at one another. 'They'll upset if they don't watch out.'

But the wing had sunk into the bottomless place, and the two canoes now made for home.

'Light's failing,' Ian said. 'We'd better go. You say your dad didn't see the thing, but only the cloud after it had gone?'

'I'm sure he didn't, because it was gone before I heard the cabin door. And besides, he looked up and said it was only the cloud of tomorrow's wind.'

'Well, if none of them saw, it's best not to tell them. They would only get steamed up. Okay?'

'Okay. But he heard that loud click when you closed the nose of the Cadillac machine. I'm just afraid he'll notice something missing. Then we *will* be in trouble. Or I will.'

'No evidence,' Ian said. 'The only evidence is on this floor in this high treetop.'

'It isn't just that. He suspects I'm seeing you again. I know he does.'

'He may only be afraid of that, like mine is. Of all their old Lord's commandments, it's the one.'

'So I'll have to tell lies and double lies and more lies, and sooner or later he'll catch me out.'

'The best way to fool him is to simply spit with hate whenever my name is mentioned, and I can do the same about you.'

'Mummy doesn't like me spitting. She says nice young ladies never spit.'

'After you, young lady.'

Mary climbed down. She minded it much less the second time. 'I know one thing,' she said at the foot.

'That's good news.'

'Shut up! What I know is that I sure hate hating. Hating's crazy.'

'Yeah, hating stinks.'

Mary's father had not forgotten his suspicions. He went up to the West Ravine next morning and spent a long time there while Mary fed her chickadees. 'Toil,' he said sadly, passing the apple tree again. 'What is life but barren toil?'

'I'll help you, Daddy.' She went to help him hill potatoes, which were sprouting. He said nothing about the Cadillac machine. 'Daddy, you seem sort of sad these days.'

'Yes, Mary, I am sad.'

'Is it for lack of company, perhaps?'

'No, no, no, decidedly not. What more company would I

want than yours and Mummy's? But I think you could both be kinder to me, Mary, sometimes.'

'Yes, I know, we could. I'll try to do better, and I'll have a word with Mummy, too. Why sad, though, Daddy?'

'I am sad because I'm trapped with a neighbour who invariably provokes me into anger, yet I can't help myself.'

'I don't blame you,' Mary said. 'I think the Smiths all stink, and the worst disgusting stinker is that boy, I sure hate him.' Mary spat a good jet at a potato plant and hit it.

'Mary, spitting is not very ladylike. But has he been bothering you, that boy?'

'Good Lord, no, Daddy. If ever I see him in the distance, I just take to my heels for all I'm worth.'

'And you would tell me if he ever bothered you – is that a promise, Mary?'

'Honest Injun, Daddy. Solemn oath.'

'You've taken a heavy burden from my mind.'

It seemed that Ian's advice was good, for her father was no more suspicious than usual during that summer; and yet most evenings Mary kept watch for an hour after supper while Ian took the electric-maker right down to pieces for cleaning and began to put it together again. He hardly spoke except to mutter about the job.

It was boring being a sentry, but Mary passed the time by thinking of rhymes. Every now and then Ian would down tools for a moment and say: 'Well, what's the latest?'

> ' "Said I to my mate:
> I sure hate hate.
> Said my mate to me:
> I do agree." '

'Not too bad,' he said. 'Not one of your best.' And he went back to work in his house which swayed and creaked when the wind was strong, and usually a small voice of wind would speak in the tree about them. It was peaceful. It was boring. It was lovely. 'Well, what's the latest?'

> ' "If Parker was white
> And Smith was darker
> Could the Lord at night
> Tell Smith from Parker?" '

'That's better,' Ian said. 'I like that one.' He chuckled to himself.

It was when the corn was ripe, and the tomatoes, and already evenings were drawing in that Ian said: 'I'll have to go to the Cadillac machine just one more time. I need to draw some oil from the belly – that's easy. And I need two gears to make it go faster – I know where they are, easy. And I need one electric eye from the nose – that's easy too, but he might miss it.'

The raid was made in the hour sacred to Daddy's snooze. But after Ian had slipped away safely, Mary sat on with the chickadees, and she was thinking that if the stories were true – and how could you know what stories were true? – if the stories were true, then in Times Before there had been millions of chickadees everywhere Outside, but now there were only these few families in the one valley, living and nesting and loving and dying. Or did chickadees live and nest and love and die far away up North in the Eskimo land? 'I just don't know anything,' she said, hearing the cabin door open and close.

Her father looked first down the lake; then turned and saw her. 'Goodbye, Chickadees,' she said, hung the suet back on the wire, and walked down to meet him. Oh, Lord! she thought, seeing the black look. He was always gloomy, but not that black look. Why?

'You were feeding your birds, Mary?'

'Yes. The whole family came, the five young ones too.'

'But this is not your usual hour to feed the birds.'

So that was it, and that was true. She had not fed them after supper since . . . 'I'm not like you,' she said. 'I don't do every single thing at the same single minute every single day.'

He ignored her, and continued on his way to the West Ravine. My fault, Mary thought. Sure as hell he'll notice that electric eye is missing. Would she escape to the woods? No, that would seem more suspicious.

Her large and comfortable mother was knitting by the stove, gave her one quick glance, and went on knitting. 'Mary dear, you look upset. What is it?'

'Just Daddy again. He's gone off snooping with a dirty look. He's sure to think up something wrong at the Cadillac machine. Then who gets blamed? He's so queer and different nowadays. Daddy used to be quite fun.'

'Daddy used to be quite fun in every way a wife would want. He was always serious underneath, but so kind, and full of pokes, oh my, and pokey jokes.' Mummy sighed.

'Well, I haven't seen him even smile for ages. What's the point of anything if everything is awful?'

'Wisely spoken, Mary. When I was young, your granny used to talk often, as you know, about the old days. She said that in Times Before there was a strange disease called a Depression, and almost all suffered it at one time or another. It was caused by the terrible helter-skelter of their lives, and there were special doctors for it who could shrink the suffering head by extracting long confession, or with pills, even with shocks from the electric, so your granny said. But we have no pills now, and no electric.'

Not that you know of, Mary thought. 'But Daddy doesn't go helter-skelter. He goes quite slowly doing every single thing at the same single moment every single day, I was just saying it to him. Could that be a reason that puts Daddy in the dumps?'

'He is at a difficult age, dear child. Your granny used to say that a man around the turn of fifty often wearies of the old girl of his lifetime and longs for fresh pastures. But such are denied to your poor daddy. But Mary, I think there are many causes – guilt for a bloody crime, fear of discovery and punishment, particularly since a part of that flying machine came floating up. What other evidence might come floating up, and when? And then all his life he has hoped and prayed that the pink ocean would turn to blue and it never does, and he is still a prisoner in a great dead deadly world.'

'But Mummy, that's been just the same for you, and you don't go moping all around the place.'

'I'm a woman, Mary. We don't go prod-prod-prodding out of vanity. We accept. But, as I was saying, many things may have brought this melancholy to your father; but to that melancholy is now added something dangerous indeed – a life-long dislike for his neighbour has turned to hatred.'

> ' "Said I to my mate:
>   I sure hate hate.
>   Said my mate to me:
>   I do agree." '

Mary's rhyme, not one of her best, slipped out somehow, and she turned her foolish back to her mother and looked out of the window, idiot.

'Where did you learn that jingle, Mary?'

'I made it up just to have a laugh about their stupid hating.'

'You laugh often nowadays. It makes me so happy to hear you laugh again.' Her mother sighed. 'I wish my mate would laugh with me.'

'Here he comes,' Mary said. 'He looks as if he's in the wildest rage.'

'Go to your room, then, dear. Go quickly!'

Mary waited there, her outside door open in case she had to run for it.

'. . . I come out from my evening nap, and I look uphill and

what do I see? I see my daughter feeding chickadees as innocently as any ewe-lamb, and I say to myself: When was it
that I last saw my daughter innocently feeding chickadees at
this hour of day? And I remember, and suspicions cross my
mind, and I go at once to the Cadillac machine whence a noise
had come that other time, and what do I find? I find a pool of
oil beneath its belly; I find a gaping hole in its chest. Then I
find – do you know what I find?'

'James, dear, I can't know until you tell me. Now calm
yourself and tell me.'

'I will not calm myself. I find that a second of the four glass
eyes in the nose of the Cadillac machine has been removed.
Where it was all my life, there is this evening an aching
void . . .'

'But James, all our lives two of the glass eyes of the Cadillac
machine have been aching voids. Didn't our mummies tell us
long ago that those eyes were shattered by the bullets of those
wicked people?'

'One was shattered, not two.'

'Two, I tell you. Mary dear!'

'Yes, Mummy?'

'How many of the four eyes of the Cadillac machine are
empty sockets?'

'Two, of course, Mummy. They always have been.'

'There! You see, James, you were mistaken. So often our
eyes play us tricks. And as for the oil and the gaping hole,
there have been drips and holes ever since I remember.'

Her father glared at Mary. He was a terrifying stranger.
'You weren't innocently feeding chickadees,' he said. 'You
were keeping watch against the enemy, your father.'

'James, you're beside yourself. While you were snoring in
your chair, I said to Mary: *Are the young chickadees feeding yet
from your hand?* And she replied: *Almost, Mummy, I'll go and
try again.* So much for keeping watch against you.'

Mary's father slumped into the chair, put his head in his hands, and groaned. His hair was nearly white, and his hands were seamed and gnarled with toil. 'Never mind, Daddy,' Mary said. She felt sorry for him, cheating him.

He looked up at her, and he said, not angrily now: 'You have been seeing the Smith boy, I know you have.'

'That bastard!' Mary said. She spat a good one at the stove. It sizzled.

'Mary, really!' Mummy said.

'Oh Lord,' he said. 'Even my own womenfolk are turned against me. Help me, Lord!' He left the cabin.

'Has he gone?'

'Yes, down by the lake.'

'We live in danger with him, Mary.'

'I know that, Mummy.'

'You must be much more careful, both of you. Now run along.'

'Mummy, you're super.' Mary ran along.

12

IAN turned his water wheel, and the big gear on that shaft turned a small gear on the second shaft, and the second shaft turned a third shaft very quickly, and on the end of the third shaft was the electric-maker from the Cadillac machine. It hummed. 'You turn it,' he said. 'I want to test.'

Mary turned the wheel for him. He licked his finger and laid it across two screws. 'Tingle-tingle, yes, I feel it. Now you try.'

She felt a small tingle along her wet finger between the screws. 'Gosh, yes,' she said. 'It really works.'

'Don't know yet,' he said. 'Now here's what you do: Unwind the handle slowly, and I'll guide it down between the branches. When it's on the ground, give me some more cable so I can put the wheel in that fastest bit of water. Then you keep watch while I run the test. If there's an alarm, I'll tell you when to wind up. Are you strong enough?'

'Of course I'm strong enough. What d'you take me for?'

'I take you for a darned good scout,' Ian said, and he laughed at her, his blue eyes bright. Always so calm and careful, and now excited about his great invention. 'Okay, let's go.'

'You sure are bossy,' Mary said, and she obeyed orders. When there was no more weight on the handle, and she had given the extra bit of cable, she stood at the window again. 'All clear,' she said. The valley was golden with goldenrod. Same colour, she thought. And there were wild asters flowering, the same pale blue as her sweater, new dyeing process, his idea, new sweater, not that he ever noticed.

She heard two sounds now, the splashing of the wheel, the hum of the electric-maker. 'Look, Mary!'

She knelt at the door, looking down. The height no longer bothered her. Ian was pointing the electric eye up to here, and it was not a dead thing of glass, but a light, a far stronger light than their fat lamps at home. 'Oh, whoopee!' she called too loudly, it was so exciting, so lovely for him after all those months of work.

'S'ssh!'

Mary went back to sentry duty in time to see their fathers hastening uphill. 'Alarm, Ian, quick!' My fault again, she thought. *Calm, lassie*! he often growled at her in his absent, kindly way. I'm a sort of stupid joke to him, she thought. And that's what I am.

'Haul away!'

Mary wound the handle. It was heavy work. She knelt at the door, winding as Ian guided his invention between the branches. Then it was in, and Ian too. 'Phew!' he whispered. 'That was a close one.'

The two men passed on either side. They were two men searching. 'Mary!' called the one. 'Ian!' called the other. Then each saw his enemy across the brook. Each turned and hastened from his enemy.

'I'm sorry, Ian,' Mary said when those strange hating men were on open fields.

'Stupid,' he said, going back to work. 'Why d'you have to get so excited and shout like that?'

'I'll tell you why – because all you ever do is boss me around and make me be sentry until I'm bored half crazy with being sentry until I could scream and so I did and so I'm stupid but I'm not stupid like you are crazy about that stupid machine and if you want to hate me go ahead.'

'Hate you?' Ian said, puzzled. 'But you're my pal. You're

the only pal I ever had. When I say stupid, I mean you're my pal. And if I'm stupid, sorry! Okay?'

'Okay, my pal,' she said.

'You might pass over that wrench, the square one.'

She passed it over. He did not bother to look up, but held his hand out for it, and touched her hand by mistake. The wrench clattered to the floor.

'Gosh!' Ian said, looking at his hand, and at her hand. 'Did you feel that?'

'Like the electric ten times over, sure I felt it right up my arm. You must be loaded with the electric from that machine.'

'Here, try again.' He held out his hand, fingers spread, and she touched the tips of his fingers with her own. 'It's you,' Ian said. 'I can feel it from you to me.' He stared at her.

'I feel it from you to me,' she said. 'Could it be from both of us?'

He went on staring at her with a new shy look. 'You're bonny,' he said. 'You're the bonniest lassie in all the world.'

'And you're the best-looking boy,' she said. 'And your hair is like the goldenrod.'

Ian shook his head. 'I must be daft. I knew you were bonny, but I never sort of noticed.'

'You were too busy with that machine to sort of notice anything.' But Mary had noticed. It had grown with her day after day and moon after moon through the long summer keeping watch beside him.

'Hang on! I've got a present for you.' And he was gone.

He had not given her a present since they were childhood friends. Was it a sin to be still as good friends as they used to be, and more? But who cared what sin might be?

'I saw it in a wet place by the brook when I was coming up, and I stopped to look at it for some reason, and here's the reason, to go in your hair.'

'A Cardinal Flower,' Mary said. 'Oh, lovely! Could you put it in for me?'

Ian put it in for her. 'Black as the night,' he said. 'Red as the Cardinal Flower.' Then he kissed her lips. It was so kind. It was so true.

The sun had sunk nearly to dead hills in the West. 'I must go, Ian. I absolutely must go now.'

'Can you get out at night?'

'That's the only safe time. It isn't safe even after supper now. But at night he passes out like some old log.'

'Tomorrow, then, when the moon comes up. And we'll bring sheepskins to keep us warm.'

'I'll keep you warmer than any sheepskin,' Mary said. 'Goodbye.'

The sun was setting beyond dead hills as she walked slowly home, and the world was new, the world was a place that she had never seen.

But Mary heard her mother's voice, and the voice of Ian's mother. 'They meet every evening somewhere in the woods, I'm sure of that.'

'Yes, and why wouldn't they be meeting?'

'It's only natural that they should still be friends as they were when they were children. And it's only natural that what will happen soon will happen.'

'You mean, they'll mate together?'

'Yes, and no Lord's commandment is going to stop them. But if James knew about our son and daughter, he would kill your Ian, I'm sure of it.'

'And Robert, he might even kill the lassie.'

'Life is becoming unbearable, Janet.'

'Yes, that's the truth of it, but what can we do?'

'All we can do is warn our children to be careful.'

'Do we warn the young bull to be careful not to mount the heifer?'

Ian's mother chuckled, and so did Mary's, coarse old females. She felt herself blushing and went on home and straight to bed. Tomorrow night she would be joined in love with Ian. It was all that she had been born for, all that she had grown for, all that she longed for.

'The light makes an extra risk. We don't need a light.'

'Just this first time. I want to see you. Do you mind me seeing you?'

'No,' Mary said. 'I want to see you too.'

He put the water wheel in the brook, and climbed again. The light hung from a nail. 'It's a super invention,' Mary said. 'But it blinds my eyes. I can't even see you properly.'

Ian turned the light to shine on the roof.

'That's lovely now,' she said. 'I brought us two apples. Let's share one, shall we?'

They sat on his sheepskin blanket, and hers round them, leaning against the wall, sharing a juicy red apple. Through the open window Mary saw the pale half moon, and a night wind swayed the tree house a little, but the wind was falling. Down there the splashing and the hum went on.

'You taste of apples,' Ian said.

'So do you.' But that apple was finished. 'Do the Eskimos have trees?'

'He said they didn't.'

'Then no other people are warm together in a tree house anywhere in the whole wide world.'

'There's no one else in the whole wide world,' he said. 'Just us.' And he began to love her, and she to love him.

It was a tremendous bang, or it was two bangs together. BANG or BANG–BANG. It was hard and painful, like slaps on both ears, and the tree house shook. 'Gosh, what was that?'

There was another sound now, a low rumble in the North. They turned their heads to listen, but it was dying, it had gone.

'Not like the flying machine,' Ian said. 'That was like far-off bumble bees. This was more like a thunder rumble.'

'But the stars are shining everywhere,' she said. And then Mary heard her own name called: 'Mary! Where are you, Mary?'

'Put the light out, Ian! Quick!'

The light was out. 'Too late,' Ian said, and his voice was calm, his arm round Mary's shoulders. 'I hear them coming. They must have seen it when they were listening to the North. Put your sweater on, Mary,' he said.

She found it in the darkness, but soon her eyes saw a little by the moon. 'I'm scared. They'll kill us.'

'No, they won't.'

The men arrived panting. 'Did you hear that explosion, Neighbour?'

'Ay, Neighbour. And did you see the light, up there it was?'

'I saw it, Neighbour.' They were polite to one another.

'My daughter was not in her bed.'

'My son was not in his.' Silence, a deadly silence but for the splashing and the hum, then women's voices.

'Robert! Come back, Robert?'

'Och, hud yer whissht, wumman!' bellowed the uncouth Scotsman.

'James! Come home at once!'

'Silence, woman!' bellowed James Parker. 'And what is this invention of the devil spinning?'

'I'll take the axe to it.'

'You will do no such thing. It is mine. The parts are mine from the Cadillac machine. Ah, ha! Now I understand her treachery. And those electric ropes leading up the tree. You are there, you slut of a daughter!'

'Yes, we're here,' Ian said. 'Shut up and go home, you daft old men. And if you take an axe to my water wheel, I'll take an axe to you.'

'Seducer! White pig!'

'Black whoore!'

There were grunts, heavings, curses as the two men climbed, Parker first, Smith at his heels. 'I'll let the first one on the ladder,' Ian muttered, peering down, the top of the ladder in his hands, waiting, then twisting with all his strength.

'Oh, Lord!' James Parker cried, falling on his enemy.

'Oh, Lord!' cried Robert Smith, at the impact of his enemy.

Crashings, gruntings, splinterings and smashings, thud upon thud, and silence. There was a finality of silence far below. 'I'll have to look.' Ian put on the light. His father's head had struck a rock; her father's head was wrongly twisted. 'Terrible,' he said. 'But what could I do?'

'They would have killed us,' Mary said.

Their mothers came, and stood in the beam of Ian's new invention.

'My James, my poor poor James!'

'My Robert, my poor poor Robert!'

The widows sobbed in the quiet night, but soon they went away.

'We can't get down until there's daylight,' Ian said. So they sat a sad while in the tree house high above the bodies of their fathers. But life was here. Ian and Mary shared a second apple and loved one another all that night and buried their fathers in the morning.

13

'I'll call when I'm ready,' Ian said.

'Will it take us long?'

'Well, it might.'

'Then I'd better leave Hamish with his grannies.'

He looked down at their son, still asleep. 'Wee man,' he said. He kissed Mary and went to the door. 'Fog again. It'll soon burn off.'

He could see a short distance down the lake. That way, the fog had a faint glow of pink in it, as always with fine weather fog. Their mothers' voices sounded from the other shore, never stopped talking, never. If there was just a man to be with sometimes. He shook his head to shake away that fed-up feeling. There were things to do.

The pipe ran over the high ridge and down again, and then climbed to a pool below the tree house. It was not one length of pipe, but a mixture of different pieces left over from Times Before – black rubbery stuff and metal lengths, and joining them had been difficult. But that was all done except at two places. He broke through quite suddenly from fog to sunshine, to look down on a field of woolly snow which hid the valley below a rim of sunlit hills. Is it really there? he thought about the hidden lake. But he heard the women gassing at the farm where he had grown up, and he heard Mary's young voice as she talked to Hamish, taking him to his grannies. The woolly snow of fog was pink beyond the waterfall.

Will it never end? thought Ian Smith. He had that thought every day, but he did not speak of it to Mary because he knew that Mary's hope was just the opposite. She said it in different ways that meant the same. She was saying it now as she sang a snatch of a song down there to Hamish in the fog. 'My Lordy lies over pink ocean . . .' she was singing. '. . . Please keep, oh please keep, oh please keep my Lordy from me.' She said it in sleepy times in bed: 'I'm so happy I don't want anything to change, not ever.'

He had laid a short length of pipe into the pool and had packed it with blue clay. There were no leaks; the water flowed clearly and strongly. Now the join here, and the one below. He spun his stick for a smoulder, blew on it, and the birchbark caught into flame to heat and soften the black pipe. He clamped with wire, no leaks.

Ian sat a while beside the brook in the perfect morning high up here. He felt good now with his small new invention, if it would work. Sometimes they did, and sometimes they didn't. That was the fun of it. Their mothers still talked, but in Granny tones, oatmeal cookies for Hamish.

The tree house was a little way uphill from him. Ian did not feel sorry for what he had done to his father and Mary's father. What else could you do to crazy old men when they were trying to kill you? 'I do miss Dad, though,' he said, and ran downhill to leave his restless thoughts behind.

Mary was picking wild strawberries in the fog. She had made a box with the big leaves of the striped maple. At that kind of neat-handed fashioning she was much better than he was. She looked up now, and smiled. She had her mother's face, narrowing to the chin, a thoughtful face that came alive with happiness. 'You're bonny,' he said. 'And that reminds me. I wish you'd sing the old words to that song. I'm fed up with the LPO.' He said it as a joke, not quite. 'Go on, sing it for me.'

Mary sang 'My Bonny lies over the ocean', picking strawberries. Her singing was another lovely thing. 'Stay away from us, LPO,' she said. 'That's all I care about. And your invention is all you care about. Is it ready?'

'We just have to fill these pipes. You hold them, I fill them, then we join them.'

'I don't see how water can flow uphill.'

'I don't either, but it does, as long as there's no air in the pipe, and as long as the place it starts from is higher than where it ends. I found out by mistake. You wait and see.'

'Okay,' she said, laying down her strawberries.

Ian filled the sheepskin bag and came up again from the lake. It was here at this rise which crossed the field between the hill and their cabin that the water would have to climb. He had to make several trips before the long pipe to the cabin was filled. The other pipe was already full as far as the hollow.

'There!' he said, when both ends stayed brimming. 'Now this is the tricky thing, not to let air in, except a tiny amount.' He took the two black pipes from Mary, one with a coupling to slide into the other. It was a tight fit, and he forced them together with all his strength.

Mary giggled. 'Now they're mates,' she said. She was always thinking of it.

He gave his mate a spank on the bottom, and her hand reached to caress him, that smile on her face, that light soft hand, both hands, smile gone, four hands, and they were naked. They made love on the wet grass in the fog. Fiercely as now, or in the lazy night, or any time.

'I'll just check for leaks uphill,' he said. 'Back soon.' Mary laughed at him, and he ran, tucking in his sheepskin kilt. His father used to call it the kilt, Mary's father the loincloth. *It's funny*, she said once. *You're more like my daddy, sort of careful. And I'm more like yours, sort of careless.* But that was long ago before their fathers became unhappy and full of hate.

The pipe glistened wet from the coldness in it, but he found no leak at any join. Ian was starting down to test his latest invention when he heard a sound.

It was a sound much like the buzzing of the bumble bee that went from rose to rose beside him. The noise grew, and the flying machine came into sight. It flew down the west side of the valley, not far beyond and not far above the rim of hills that rose from fog. It was the same mustardy colour and the same stubby shape as another flying machine before. It flew on over the pink fog of the ocean, the sound dying, almost gone, not gone. The droning moved East and grew again. This time the machine flew up the Smith side of the valley where their mothers now lived.

The sound dwindled to the North. Ian had not moved since first he heard it. He stood in sunlight, not able to move or not thinking to move except to turn, to watch, to listen a full circle. He heard his heart thump in the great excitement of what he had wanted for so long.

But the flying machine was coming a third time, headed straight for him. Had it seen him? Wave? Hide? He could not think, but his legs or something said to him: *Hide*! And he dived for cover. The flying machine roared overhead, turned away, turned North. This time the sound died altogether.

He ran down to Mary. She faced up the valley, her hands to her cheeks, her mouth trembling.

'It was the same, just like the other one.'

She flung her hands down. Not so long ago those slender hands had touched him. 'Did they see you?'

'I don't think so. I didn't know rightly what to do, but I hid when it came near me. They couldn't see the valley for fog.'

'If not today, tomorrow, they'll be down, or some tomorrow after tomorrow. That's what you've always wanted, isn't it?'

'No,' he said. 'Not always, I don't know. I did want to see a flying machine.'

'For more lovely inventions, I suppose.' She was angry. Mary afraid was Mary angry. 'Well, let's go and try out your stupid invention.' She started to run to the cabin, but walked again.

'You've forgotten the strawberries.' He picked up her box of leaves. 'Don't you want water at the cabin, just to turn the tap and have all the water you could need? Is that a stupid invention?'

'I'm sorry,' she said, waiting for him. She was crying. 'I'm the stupid one, not your invention. Of course I want it.'

He put his spare arm round Mary's bare shoulders. The fog was going quickly now. It went quickly from cool quietness to warm sun. 'Go on, great inventor, turn the tap.'

'You turn it,' he said. 'That would bring us better luck.'

Mary tried to turn it. 'The other way, stupid,' he said. She laughed at herself or at him, and caught her breath after tears, and turned it the other way.

The water rushed out in a hard straight jet. 'Gosh, it works!'

'Let it run until we're sure.' The water was a dirty brown, and there were gasps and splutterings, but then it ran firmly. After a long while it began to clear.

'Just think!' she said. 'No more water to fetch.'

'Only in summer,' he said, but he was thinking on. He was thinking that if he got one of the old tubs from the junkpile, and set it in the pasture, and extended this pipe, then the cattle could drink up there, not dirty the shore of the lake. '. . . What, Mary?'

'I was saying that if it was the same kind of flying machine, they'll be the same kind of people.'

'I guess so. I don't quite see why.'

'So what about when they ask what happened to the other ones?'

'Oh, Lord,' he said. 'I never thought of that.' There were suddenly a hundred things that he had never thought of.

'You were too busy,' she said, not angrily but coldly. 'Do we say our fathers chopped their heads off?'

'Don't be stupid. There's no sign of them left, not a single thing.'

'Not until another bit pops up from the bottom of the lake. What then?'

'I don't know,' he said. 'I don't know anything.'

'If you don't know anything, I know double nothing.'

'We'd better talk to our mums. They're pretty sensible.'

'Yes, they're pretty sensible. Let's go.'

Their mothers kept the poultry, grew the vegetables, sewed winter skins, and knitted. Ian and Mary farmed and worked in the woods. Or that was the general way of things. But everyone shared now in the valley. There was a sadness that happiness had come in the way that it had come. But what about happiness tomorrow?

They went by canoe, which was the quicker way, past the end of No-Man's-Island where they had had the feast that other time, how long ago? We were ten, Ian thought. And we're nineteen now.

The sun was hot, and he was sweating, and Mary's brown back glistened as she drove her paddle strongly. It was haying time again, flying machine time again, so much to think about, and they grounded on the shore.

For once their mothers were not talking. They weeded apart, at each end of a row of peas, but they straightened, staring at him.

'I saw it,' he said. 'It was the same as the other one, same colour and everything.'

'They'll be back,' Ruth Parker said.

'Ay, they'll be back,' said Janet Smith.

Both women turned, their lined faces anxious, to look down the lake to the place where the first machine had been sunk.

Then they looked at him. 'You tell us, Ian,' they said together and Mary was watching him too.

'Did the Eskimos say it was a long way to the next blue lake?'

The three women nodded.

'So they may have gone back for more of that gasoline stuff they use, and they can't come until the fog has gone, so tomorrow is more likely than today. But we must be ready for them, and we must seem glad to see them.' Now he was thinking straighter at last.

The three women nodded.

'A feast, then. I'll lay a fire right away on No-Man's-Island to have it ready. And the lamb is easy when the time comes. All that's no problem. But what are we to say about the flying machine? Those first ones could have reported on the radio that they were here. Or perhaps these ones will see it lying in the bottomless place. Or perhaps that other time it was a flying machine miles up high that could have seen down through the water to it.'

'What other time?'

'We never told you,' Mary said. 'We thought you – I mean, they – would only get steamed up.' And she explained about the pencil of cloud that had crossed the sky.

'When was it?'

'It was three years ago. It was that summer.'

Their mothers, who were so contented and such good friends, could not think of their men without pain. Most of the time it lay deeply for them now; yet rose more strongly. But Hamish, who had been sleeping in the shade, awoke, and his grannies soon cheered up, taking turns to hold him.

I mustn't seem worried, Ian thought. '. . . Mary, you're the best one at welcoming – just be cheery, and I'll help with the ropes and things, and we'll all be really pleased to see them. And don't get excited, Mary. You say such daft things when you get excited.'

'Okay,' she said. 'Mum's the word. The Mums can do the talking.'

'The *listening*,' Ian said. 'We'll let them speak first, and find out what they know. And if they ask awkward questions, just play stupid until I have time to think.'

'The other ones called us untutored savages. Which is what we are, eh Janet?'

'That's right, Ruth. It'll be like second nature, playing stupid.'

The old girls chuckled, but briefly. The unknown lay heavy on the minds of all except the youngest member.

'They may not come,' Ian said. But in spite of all the dangers which he had never thought properly about before, he would be disappointed if these Eskimos did not come in their flying machine. 'Who knows if they'll come?'

'Who knows?'

He stood, and swung Hamish up to sit astride his head, and ran a bit to make him laugh. At nearly two, he was a strong and happy boy, with a grand fierce temper in him too, just like his mother.

'If they do come,' he said on the way across the lake, 'you'd better put on a sweater. They had queer notions about that, remember?'

'Yes,' she said. 'And I remember how he married them and baptized us. Wouldn't you like to be baptized, Hamish?'

'As if it mattered,' Ian said, but she said nothing.

The flying machine did not return that day.

They made a start with haying in the afternoon. Ian had managed to repair the haymower which had rusted away in the Smiths' junkpile all these years. In three or four days now, with the oxen and the mower, he could do what had taken their fathers and mothers as many weeks by hand. To Mary's father and to Ian's father, anything simple like a plough was all right, and a wheeled wagon was all right; but a machine with complicated gears was an invention of the devil. Mysterious madness, Ian could never understand that, although he knew where it came from. It came from Mary's grandfather, the Morley one, the famous biologist one, her mother's father who preached that man's inventions were out of his control, and would destroy the world for sure.

But he knew that, with a part of her, Mary felt that too. She said how wonderful the haymower was, and the electric to the cabin, and the water now. But she feared even simple things like those.

'I'm scared of them coming,' she said in the dark in bed.

'So am I,' he said. 'Well, half scared, it'll be all right.' But he looked forward to the flying machine, perhaps even gasoline. His steam machine was difficult.

'Perhaps they know everything, and they'll come with guns to shoot us for what our fathers did to them.'

'Our mothers are scared too,' Ian said. 'But it'll be all right. You'll see.'

'A flying machine for your very own. That's what you want, isn't it?'

'Now you're being stupid,' Ian said.

'It's different for a man. For me it's just not wanting anyone or anything ever but you.'

'Not even wee Hamish?' he said, teasing her. And soon they slept together.

14

NEXT morning the fog was thicker and did not clear all day. Sometimes the fog would stay right through the growing and the dying of a summer moon. Perhaps it would be that kind of fog, hanging over the pink ocean and the land.

There were always more things to do than Ian had time for. He worked away in the quiet weather, and Mary worked with him. She was as good as a man at helping to build a snake-fence, better than Ian himself at light-handed jobs. It was only in the heaviest labour with rock or log that he missed the strength of another man.

But that day gave him more time to think about the Eskimos, to plan what to do and say if they should come.

'They may not come,' he said, hoping that they would.

'Of course they'll come,' she said, hoping that they would not. Mary was gloomy and rather bad-tempered, not like her joking self.

But during the second night a breeze blew from the North and West to drive the fog away. It was hot by mid-morning, perfect for haying.

They were having a quick cool swim before dinner, Hamish with them – he loved to splash in shallows – when the sound came again. It grew and faded in the West.

'You take the small canoe, and embers to light the fire, that's quicker. I'll look after Hamish, and get the lamb.'

'Light it now?' she said. 'But they may not come.'

Of course they'll come. They may not come. 'We must be ready,' he said. 'And if they don't come, we can always make another for when they do. Don't forget your sweater.'

Ian slaughtered, cleaned and skinned the lamb. Now Hamish sat between his legs in the canoe, and he was crying. 'Never mind, wee man,' Ian said. 'Never mind.'

Hamish bawled for hunger or for a tooth or if he did not get his way, but briefly. 'What's the matter?' Mary asked, taking him.

'He didn't like me killing the lamb. But what could I do?' Ian never killed now except for food.

'Baa–lamb,' Hamish sobbed in Mary's arms, but soon he was quiet. 'Have a snooze before the feast,' she said, putting him in a shady place away from the fire, which had blazed mightily but now settled to deep hot ashes for perfect cooking.

Their mothers came with pots for boiling this summer's first new potatoes and baby peas. They wore upper garments. They joined Mary and Hamish in the shade, but neither spoke.

'You can't wear those,' Ian said. 'Those are the Mother Hubbard things the Eskimos brought you for decency. Think! We must all think. Now go and change at once.'

The old girls, muttering self-reproaches, hurried to obey him, each wielding a paddle.

Bully them, something said to him. 'And cheer up,' he called. 'I don't want to see any more sad faces.'

'We know nothing, Mary,' he said. 'Nothing about the Eskimos except what they tell us, nothing about the World Outside or Times Before or anything except what our parents told us. Have you got that fixed in your bonny head?'

'Muddled head,' she said. 'It's all so muddling. I mean, for instance, suppose they ask what happened to our fathers?'

'Our fathers had an accident in the woods. That's true. But if you must tell whoppers, Mary Parker, make them as strong as whoppers can be.'

'It's wrong to tell whoppers, Ian Smith,' she said, and they laughed together.

'Listen!' But it was only the wind of haying time. 'The lamb will spoil in this heat. We'd better cook it anyway.' And he set about doing that. 'Let's have a quick swim,' he said when it was sizzling just right.

They dived and climbed out to dry in the sun. The canoe was coming back. 'I'm Mary Smith,' Mary said. 'That's my proper name, not Mary Parker. And it will be soon, if they marry us like Jesus. But you think that's silly.'

'H'mm,' he said.

'H'mm,' she copied him.

He escaped the argument she wanted by going to turn the lamb a last time. The potatoes were boiling, and the peas, feast almost ready.

'I hear it,' Mary said. The sound grew quickly, and the flying machine skimmed over the hills. It circled the valley, as the other one had done, and came low over the waterfall, almost touching, almost, touching now, throwing up twin columns of spray. The machine sank deeper, and the roar changed to splutterings, but gathered once more as it swam towards them, ungainly creature.

It was all the same as last time until the spinner slowed to a stop at the middle of the lake near the bottomless place, and the flying machine rocked gently, turning.

'They must know it's sunk there.'

'S'ssht!' Ian said. 'Stand up. Give them a cheery wave.'

Something moved at the side, a window sliding. Would they hear the guns and the bullets coming?

But no gun banged, and no bullets came. The machine rocked in the small waves of the haying wind, drifting down the lake until the spinner started again with coughs, and it moved this way.

'Now remember,' Ian said. 'Mary and I do the welcoming. Then we have the feast right away, too busy eating for much talk. But we listen to what they say, and you Mums answer the easy questions. But be careful, and if you're stuck, play stupid to give us time to think.'

The flying machine stopped near shore, and a man climbed down on to one of the floats, a rope coiled in his hand. He had a pale face and dark hair, a thin man, not at all like those ruddy square Eskimos. 'Hullo,' he said, unsmiling, and threw the rope.

'Speak up!' Ian muttered, stooping for the end.

'Hi, there! Greetings!' Mary's voice went high, but she continued: 'Welcome to join us at our haying feast. You're just in time for roast fatted lamb and new potatoes and baby peas.'

The man did smile then, but briefly, as if a smile would be dragged from him. 'Fasten to that tree,' he said. It was the same tree as the Eskimo time. He ran the other end of the rope through a ring on each float and drew it through, and tossed the coil to Ian. 'Now you can haul us in.'

Ian did as he was bidden. It was all the same, and all so strict and different from the kindly laughing Eskimos. The man came ashore, and a woman stepped from the cabin to the float to follow him. She had a friendly smiling face, perhaps not so different. She raised her right hand and said: 'May the dear Lord bless you.'

'Better introduce myself,' the man said in a short sharp way. 'I am Curtis George Third, and this is my wife, the Reverend Annabel George.'

Curtis George, Ian thought. Curtis George. Didn't the Eskimo say that name?

'And that's my mother, Mrs Parker,' Mary said. 'And that's Ian's mother, Mrs Smith, and this is Ian Smith and I'm Mary Parker, and this is our son, Hamish.' Mary spoke in a rush. First mistake, Ian thought. Our Mums were never Mrs until the Eskimos married them. But perhaps it didn't matter.

'Welcome to our valley and our feast,' said Ruth Parker.

'It's a real pleasure to be meeting you,' said Janet Smith.

Everyone except Hamish made small bows, and nobody shook hands. The man and the woman wore shirts and long trousers of a pale brown colour, dressed alike except that above her left breast there was a small black cross.

'Let's start,' Ian said. 'The lamb is just right.' He moved it to the wooden platter and began to carve. He had sharpened the worn knife to a razor edge. The woman murmured a few words about bless this good food; and then they were all eating in the shade of the old white pine beside the shore.

It was hot, and the wind was getting up. 'We should be haying,' Ian said. 'But we always have this feast at the beginning.' That was not true. The last two years they had had the feast at the end of haying, and another in the fall when the later crops were in.

'What lovely food,' the woman said. 'I've never tasted anything so good.' She laughed. 'When I compare it with what we have at home, eh, Curtis?'

The man smiled too, eating hungrily, his face less stern. Perhaps he was just a man who felt awkward at meeting new people. Ian had only once before met new people, and it was strange and frightening now. 'Where is home?' he asked the man.

Curtis George Third finished the mouthful, darted his tongue out through his lips and said: 'We live far North of here, almost two thousand miles away in Eskimo land.'

'Ess – kee – mo. Is that a place, or is it a kind of people?'

'A kind of people.'

'Are you Eskimos?' They were white people, but perhaps they were Eskimos too.

'No, we are Caucasians, the same as yourself.' He glanced directly at Ian and then at his mother, ignoring the others.

Silence again until it was time for wild strawberries and cream. 'Delicious,' the woman said. 'I remember a last can of strawberries when I was a child. You see, our supplies ran out long ago. Since then we've been living on Eskimo fare, which is rather basic.' She laughed again. She was a kind of easy person you did not feel strange with. 'Oh, what a paradise your little valley is.' She pointed across the lake. The cattle were lying down, chewing the cud, and the sheep were in a field farther up. 'Do you know that I've never seen a cow or sheep before except in pictures, and nor has my husband, have you, dear?'

'No,' he said. He was watching Mary, whose eyes had wandered again to the bottomless place. 'Have you had other visitors?' he asked abruptly.

'No,' Ian said before the others could speak. 'You're the very first people who ever came to the lake since the ones who tried to break in. They killed all our grandfathers, but our mothers were too young to remember that for themselves.' It was a big flat lie, and he thought he told it well.

'Nine years ago,' said George, his cold eyes flickering over their faces one by one. Now it was coming. 'Nine years ago an Eskimo clergyman named Noel Avakana and his wife made a last cache of gasoline three hundred miles north of here. The drums are at that lake . . .'

There were now frantic wailings from the cabin of the plane. 'Shut that child up,' said Curtis George Third, frowning.

'That is our little Susan,' said Mrs George, 'our younger daughter, I will fetch her.' She went to do so, and returned with a child of about Hamish's age, a pretty small girl with fair hair like her mother. Mrs George brought also a piece of pink fish that Ian remembered. 'This is Arctic Char, the Eskimos call it *Irkalukpik*, raw and kept frozen in our freezer, you must try it sometime. But I think your rich new food might upset Susan's little tummy. We can introduce her to it gradually.'

Susan took the fish and gobbled it. Then she and Hamish

stared at one another, and kept on staring. 'What a handsome boy he is,' said Mrs George. Her husband drew in a quick breath and said nothing.

'What a bonnie wee lassie,' said Ian's mother.

This interruption had given Ian much needed thinking time. Had they sent a radio message to the far North from here? He would have to risk it. 'A flying machine – it looked like yours – did come,' he said. 'I remember all that exactly because Mary and I were playing by the burn, and we were quite high and could see everything. It went twice round the lake, down the Parker side and up our side, and round again, and we waved and waved, and then it flew over the Lord's pink ocean. Perhaps it was going to turn and come on to the lake just like you did. But that was when it happened. Suddenly the roaring buzz became pop, pop, pop, and suddenly there was no sound at all, and we watched it sink down and down until it splashed into the sea. So we all ran, both families, to the waterfall to have a closer look. It was still quite a long way off, too far to be sure, but that afternoon we thought we saw somebody get down on the float, to try to mend the machine perhaps, and we stayed there, hoping and hoping that they would be able to fly again before the pink ocean got at them. But they never did.'

Ian was out of stories by this time, and Mary's mother took on: 'There was nothing we could do,' she said. 'So we watched all day both days until the storm began with great winds and rain, and when the storm was over, there was no flying machine. Oh, those poor people!'

Curtis George's pointed tongue pushed out, in again. '*People*. How do you know there were more than one?'

'Because you're people, aren't you?' said Mary. 'And besides, you just said that what's-his-name brought a wife.'

'Of course you said that, Curtis dear.'

'Didn't they send you a message by radio or whatever it is?'

Ian asked. 'We have things called radios in our junkpiles, and television boxes too.'

'Those would probably be receivers, not transmitters. Yes, we got a faint signal after they had taken off from the last staging point, and then no more. Communications are bad in the heat of day.' A quick lick of lips; then he rapped out: 'You have had no other visitors?'

'Ian told you that', Mary said, just as sharply.

'Wait, though. No visitors, but three summers ago . . .' And Ian told him about the pencil of cloud going over the sky from North to South. '. . . So we wondered what it could be.'

'That was our supersonic transport plane out of Thule in Greenland, equipped with auxiliary fuel tanks . . .' Curtis George explained, just as Avakana had done, about the few scientists in the Antarctic. '. . . So we shipped down four Eskimo couples and three Caucasian couples and two Negroid couples, all with young children. They were not particularly anxious to go, but I employed persuasion.'

'I don't wonder they weren't anxious to go from the beginning of our lovely Arctic spring to that fiendish Antarctic winter.' The woman clergyman shuddered. 'Seventy below zero and the wind. Fiendish,' she said.

'Annabel knows because she came along to minister to the old chaps' immortal souls. The youngest of the survivors is about seventy-seven.' There was a word for the way he spoke – sarcastic was the word.

'Couldn't you bring them up to Eskimo land if it's so much nicer?'

'A waste of fuel,' said Curtis George briefly. 'On their way out, not worth a damn to us.'

'Oh, Curtis,' his wife said, and she sighed. Hamish and Susan were having fun now, playing with pebbles. 'They're going to be friends,' she said.

'We don't discourage it as between small children.' Silence

fell but for the hot wind in the pine tree. And Ian had that dream feeling. He would wake up and it would all have been a dream. He closed his eyes and opened them. It seemed real enough, and not real. And if it was real, why had this nasty man come? *Let them do the talking*, he had said before. But there could still be many awkward questions, better say something safe before the man thought of them.

'One night later that summer we heard a terrific bang, or perhaps it was bang-bang, and then a roar going away to the North.' That bang was what really killed our fathers, Ian did not say.

'We made that noise,' said Curtis George. 'Going down, we had a tremendous tail wind, and we flew below the speed of sound to conserve fuel. But coming back with a much lighter load, we flew at fifteen hundred miles an hour. Hence the supersonic boom. It's a little difficult to explain,' he said quite nicely to Ian.

'Why didn't you come in your super-machine this time? It would only take you an hour and a bit.'

'Because the SST operates from a hard surface, not from water,' he said to Mary. 'It needs miles of smooth runways, perhaps ten of your lakes put end to end.'

'Oh, I see,' she said, silence again.

But this time Curtis George got to the question before Ian could think of anything more to say. 'Your common law husbands,' he said in that cold way to Ruth Parker and Janet Smith. 'Are they dead?'

They nodded. They could never speak of it.

'Our fathers had an accident,' Ian said. 'They were felling a giant spruce tree, and they had sawed almost right through when a sudden wind twisted the tree and it fell on them.'

'It fell on *both* of them? But that doesn't make sense.'

'They're dead,' said Ruth Parker.

'Does that make sense?' said Janet Smith. The widows walked away.

'Curtis dear, must you be so harsh?'

'I'm what I am,' he said. 'Be quiet.' And his wife was quiet, afraid of him.

'How do you know about trees falling on people when you don't even have any trees in that Eskimo land?' Now Mary was angry.

'And may I ask, young woman, how you know that we don't have any trees in that Eskimo land?'

'I'll tell you just how,' she said, not hesitating a second. 'Because in the spring before Ian and I were born, those stupid Smiths started a grass fire, and it burned everything up, the books we had and everything almost, and our fathers and mothers told us what they could remember of all those books, and one of them was about the bare Eskimo land where spring comes in the middle of the summer. That's what those Smiths did.' *Those* Smiths, *those* Parkers, not since their fathers' deaths had anyone used that word.

'*Those* Smiths,' said Curtis George thoughtfully. But he said no more. Thinking and planning, always thinking and planning, you could see it in his narrow cold-eyed face.

He was surprising too. You couldn't know what to expect next. His whole look changed now, and he said in a friendly way, 'One thing that interests me is this: You have never in your lives had books, and yet both you young people speak the English language remarkably well.'

'Do we?' Mary said, pleased.

'You do, indeed. Perhaps with limited vocabularies, but grammatically.'

'That's easy to explain,' she said. 'Both our families had grammar books and elementary arithmetic books and small dictionaries before the fire, and they had learned them off by heart. They didn't know much, but they've taught us all they knew.'

'Most interesting,' he said. 'It is a well-known phenomenon, the sharpening of the mind which has little means at its disposal, the near perfection of memory, universal among primitives, as for example, our Eskimos.'

The widows had come back. They stood sombrely, resentfully. Curtis George also stood. 'Sorry if I hurt your feelings,' he said. 'Quite unintentional.'

'May their souls rest in peace,' said Annabel George, and she made the same sign, from brow to stomach and across her breasts, as Avakana had done.

'Ian,' he said. 'Would you care to show me around? I might be able to give you a tip or two.'

'That would be great,' Ian said. There was nothing to hide, no, nothing to hide, only something hidden in the bottomless place. 'Let's go, then,' he said. They got into the canoe as Annabel George said to Mary Parker: 'The children are so hot. Wouldn't they like to splash a little in the shallow water?'

Ian paddled for shore. He would show him the water wheel and the electric first; then perhaps get some tips about that steam machine. But I must be careful, he thought. Watch every word I say. Watch for that tongue to come darting out.

15

THEY looked at the water wheel, which spun on day and night with a merry splashing. It was joined by shaft and gears to the electric-maker on the bank, and that was humming.

Curtis George inspected everything closely, but he did not ask questions, rather disappointing. Now he turned and stared down at the valley. From up here you could see it all except the farther side of No-Man's-Island where the plane floated, and the women and children were. 'It is indeed a beautiful place,' he said. 'To think that, except possibly for a few un-detectable desert nomads and the like, yours is the only sur-viving colony of human beings between the Arctic and the Antarctic.'

'How do you know that?'

'Because in the early days our observation satellites were still circling the Earth, and Thule was a monitoring station. A few thousands of us in the North, you people here, the small Antarctic colony, and much the largest, the Russians in Siberia. That is all.'

'But if there are blue lakes like the one where the gasoline is, why no people?'

'Because the blue lakes, as you call them, are few and far between to the North, a few among millions, one might say, and because almost none of those myriad lakes of the Canadian Shield were ever inhabited. It was a barren wilderness. As for any southern places like your own that might have escaped the scourge, the people would have gone out unwittingly to their deaths, or they became desperate for food and had to risk it. I wonder only how your people had the good sense to stay.'

'I think one of Mary's grandfathers persuaded them.'

'Indeed? A wiser black brother than the common run.'

He said it nastily. But most of the things he said about survivors and so on were just what that Eskimo had said.

'We have the safe lakes charted now, entirely thanks to the intrepid pioneer work of Noel Avakana, and the records he left behind. If there were only more Eskimos like that! Shall we go down, then?'

'If you follow the pipe and the wires,' Ian said, 'they'll take you to our cabin. I'll bring the canoe round.'

He ran down to the canoe, and reached the cabin at the same time as Curtis George, who turned on the tap and watched the water gushing. 'The principle of the syphon. Did someone tell you, or did you discover it yourself?'

'That was just a fluke of mine,' Ian said. 'Now would you like to see the electric?' He put on the switch. The beam was so narrow that he had it pointed at a shiny old metal plate upside down on the ceiling, and it spread back down to be a very good light after darkness, and useful even now, with only one window in the room. We pointed it up in the tree house the time you banged us, Ian thought. And . . . 'What did you say?'

'I asked: You had no books or manuals at all to work from?'

'No,' Ian said. 'I looked and looked until I could see how it must have worked, not so difficult, not like starting new.'

'I think it's extraordinary,' Curtis George said. 'Ian, you have remarkable gifts. What I wouldn't give for a few young fellows like you.' He looked at him admiringly, yet closely.

'Are you the sort of Boss man up there in the North?'

'In our own North, yes, you could call me that,' Curtis George said in his abrupt, sharp way again. He went on more slowly: 'Noel Avakana was an excellent influence with his own people, but after he disappeared, the Eskimos soon were slipping back into the shiftless anarchy which for so long had been their way of life. Also, there was much ill-feeling – even bloody clashes – between the various sections of our community, inter-breeding too.' He cleared his throat. 'I decided that someone must take firm charge and lead. So I led . . .' Curtis George talked on a bit about his North, but it was rather boring with strange words, and at the first pause Ian said: 'This is my steam machine. It's much more difficult.'

'A gasoline motor.' It was on the floor of the cabin, the bits scattered round it. 'I'm not a qualified engineer, so I can't be much help; but I imagine that the problem is timing the injection of steam under pressure into each of the four cylinders.'

'That's just it,' Ian said. 'It beats me every time, and I have no tools to make the new machineries I need.'

'How would it be if, in our next party in a week or two, I were to include one of my expert engineers with the tools you need?'

'Well, thanks,' Ian said. But how many people might be coming, be piling in?

They went outside. 'Now perhaps you could tell me a little about your farm operation.'

Ian explained how in desperation their fathers had mixed the breeds on the farm, and Curtis George nodded; he explained how they changed different crops from field to field – oats, hay, potatoes, turnips, and Curtis George nodded. 'Us Smiths were farmers,' Ian said, 'and I think the Parkers learned mostly from us, but Mary's father became a better farmer than mine.' And Curtis George nodded.

'Tell me, Ian. You spread your manure?'

'Oh, yes. We collect it from the barn all winter, and spread it in the spring.'

'I have no experience by which to judge crop quality, but barnyard manure is usually deficient in phosphorus, which stimulates flower and seed production. Also, I think these coastal soils are mostly acid, but I would suppose that you have no available sources of phosphorus or lime.'

'I don't understand those things,' Ian said. 'How do you know about them if you can't have beasts and crops up there? That's what our book said.'

'My knowledge is purely theoretical,' George said. 'But I have studied that and many other subjects thoroughly. Every moment of every day is for me a preparation.' He stared at Ian, and his eyes were gleaming, strange deep uncomfortable man. 'My scientists assure me that the time will come when the ocean and the land will stir to life again. It is for that time that I prepare myself. And you must prepare yourself, too, because you here at our southern base camp – a place of cardinal importance – you will be the first to know.'

'Base camp?'

'With more good hands and better tools, this valley would support a much larger population.'

'Oh, I see,' Ian said. But it was too much and too dangerous to see, or to think straight about.

'I plan to fly tomorrow morning to the next lake to fetch two more drums of gasoline. Handling them is heavy work for my wife, quite useless at it. Would you like to come with me?'

'Oh, gosh, yes, I would like that fine.' There was nothing in the world that he would like better, but then he remembered about haying, this day lost already. 'If the weather's decent, I should be mowing and pitching hay. Once you get behind-hand, you never seem to catch up.'

'Couldn't the girl and your mothers mow hay, and my wife would help.'

'Well, I guess so,' he said. 'Oh, gosh, okay.'

'Good. There are two drums in the plane now. Do you have a stout plank we could use to roll them down directly to the shore? That would be easier.'

'There's a plank in the woodshed, sure.' They went round

to the shed, and Ian searched through the pile of old board lumber for the thicker plank. He got down to it, and pulled out one end, and moved for the other.

Curtis George Third was standing at the door, an axe in hand, and he was staring at the head of the axe Ian used for splitting and in the woods, his better one. He stared at the square heel of it, the part facing up the handle. It was the part where the face like the man in the moon was stamped.

Ian heard his heart beat fast, and he felt dizzy, going pale, he knew. He turned quickly away to hide his face, and he wrestled with the plank until he felt better again. 'Will this do?'

'That will do splendidly,' said Curtis George politely. His face said nothing. His face was quite blank, the deadly man. 'Let me help you.'

'I can manage.' The plank weighed nearly as much as Ian himself, but he swung it up easily, and went down to the canoe. 'If you could just help me to lay it in gently. The canoe isn't very strong.'

Curtis George helped him to do that. Neither of them spoke on the way to No-Man's-Island.

Ian was working on the steam machine; but he was not really working, he was fiddling, so much to listen to and think about.

'. . . The children had a lovely time together, and she's just as sweet as she can be, but terrified of that snake, and I don't wonder. So anyway, I asked her if she would marry us to-morrow.'

'It would have to be in the afternoon. I'm flying with him for more gasoline first thing.'

'Ian, you're not! But it's dangerous.'

'They've flown all those thousands of miles again and again. How can it be dangerous?'

'I didn't mean just flying. He's what I said, a snake always watching and waiting like the grass snake in the grass, tongue flicking too.'

Ian laughed. 'Yeah, I know. But he's leaving his wife and kid here, so it's safe enough tomorrow.'

'Well, I suppose.'

'Who are they, anyway?'

'She told me that, what I could understand. His grandfather was Commanding General – soldier boss, that means – at the flying place in Greenland. And her grandfather was a clergy-man there – a chaplain, she said first. Well, food ran short, and in their father's time they moved along some Arctic coast to live with the Eskimos beside the safe cold water and the ice. So then Curtis George and Annabel fell in love – can you imagine him making love, far less falling in it? – and they were married by Noel Avakana, and when he disappeared, she be-came a clergyman because it was sort of in her family, they all loved Jesus. So now he's boss of the Eskimos and everyone up North, and she is their pastor, and she says most of the time it works beautifully.' Mary paused for breath. 'Those strange words, it's so muddling. But when I asked her about marrying us, she said: *Perhaps tomorrow, dear*, and sighed and said: *I'll have to speak to Curtis. Oh, look at the children splashing one another*! Changed the subject just like that.'

We're happy together with Hamish, Ian thought. What does marrying us matter? But he did not say it. It was dusk outside. 'Are they sleeping in a tent?'

'Yes, we helped her put it up while you were away. It's in that small open place beside the path.'

'They may still be awake. I'm going to listen.'

'Be careful, Ian.'

He went out and round by the shore, and he swam the short distance to No-Man's-Island. He had not told Mary about the axe-head. That would only frighten her. But he had never given a thought to the moon-face stamped on it. Almost everything in the junkpiles had some old stamp or mark. And yet the way Curtis George had held the axe to a better light and stared . . .

Ian's bare feet made no sound on the path. Yes, they were talking, or the man was talking, and the door of the tent faced the other way.

'. . . I knew all along they were lying in their teeth. For one thing, Ian asked whether the word Eskimo meant a kind of people or a place, but later the girl snapped back about the Eskimo book they used to have.'

Cunning beast, Ian had not even thought of that.

'He might have forgotten, dear.'

'I said it this afternoon: The unlettered peasantry never forget. But the axe-head settles it.'

'How does an axe-head settle it, dear?'

'Because Okpik, the Owl, is the trademark of the Arctic Foundry. They've always been proud of their enigmatic bird, stamped on every piece of finished metal they produce; and the Arctic Foundry was established thirty-one years ago. What other foundry ever before would have used the baleful earless face of the Snowy Owl as trademark?'

'Well, I suppose not, Curtis, but . . .'

'There are no buts to it, proof positive. Ian and the girl would have been about ten, so they are out of it, and the hags seem harmless. Their fathers murdered Avakana and his wife. Furthermore, I think I know from the way their eyes wandered – I know where they sank that plane.'

'What are you going to do about it, dear?'

'I shall do nothing and say nothing now. We must woo their confidence. In due course I shall send down one of my toughest security people to get at the truth, and that will be easy: Arrest their loved ones, a scream or two, and those old women will break in five minutes.'

'So hard and ruthless you're becoming, Curtis. Sometimes you frighten me.'

'I can't help that. My mission is clear.'

'I wish my mission seemed clearer to me.'

'How many more times am I to tell you, Annabel? Your mission is to minister to a primitive superstitious people. That is why I had you ordained. We are point and counterpoint. It is as simple as that.'

'It's not so simple to be used because of my love for Jesus.' His wife sounded bitter. 'And because of my love for you.'

'Oh, please!' he said quietly. 'Nothing but purpose can be simple.'

'Mary asked me this afternoon. What a beautiful girl she is, with that fine-chiselled face, not at all like most of our black people.'

'Of Hamitic stock, I imagine, from my reading. Yes, she is comely enough. But I wouldn't trust that sharp-tongued wench a single inch.'

'And Ian is the best-looking thing, and little Hamish is a lovely child.'

'A lovely little mulatto.'

'Happy too,' she said. 'Such a happy young family. Mary asked me this afternoon if I would marry them, and I had to stall about it.'

'You know my policy. You know that you cannot marry them.'

'But this is an exceptional case, Curtis dear. This is a unique case. They were childhood friends, she told me. They grew up together. They fell in love. You only have to look at them to know it was inevitable, to know how true and good it is.'

'Miscegenation cannot be true and good. Be careful, Annabel. If you condone miscegenation, you betray your loyalty to me.'

'Jesus said nothing about miscegenation. I don't betray my loyalty to Jesus.'

'Your Jesus is old hat, and well you know it. Only the Eskimos still believe.'

'Alas,' she said. 'Yes, alas. You won't allow this one exception?'

'I will not. If I allowed one, how many others would there be? Besides, the boy will be well cared for, happily impotent at our Arctic Orphanage.'

'Oh, God,' she said.

'Do you not realize, my good earnest woman, that Ian has never set eyes upon a beautiful girl of his own race? Suppose he were to meet our own Deborah . . .'

'I can't stand it,' Annabel said. 'You're so inhuman. I'm going out.'

Ian went quickly back the way he had come. Round the shores the yellow frogs were puffing their bellies up and going PONK.

16

THEY flew for two hours and twenty minutes over the dead grey lands and the pink waters. 'Just watch what I do, and I'll explain the instruments.' There were many things to learn, like the variable prop, altimeter, revolutions, airspeed, mixture, all of them new.

And there were others to look at in the cabin: two guns tied along the wall, an axe with a mark on it – the owl, Ian thought. 'What's this?' he asked.

'That, or those, are binoculars. They magnify, bring distant objects nearer. I inspected you through them when first we landed at the lake.'

Curtis George had answered all Ian's questions carefully and loudly in the noisy cabin. It was cool at five thousand feet.

'There!' George said. He pointed to a patch, a strip of bluish water ahead of them, slowed the engine, and pushed forward the half-wheel he held.

'This is a different kind of lake from yours, although almost certainly volcanic too. There is no inlet, nor an outlet so far as I can see. It is what we call a pothole or a giant dew-pond, fed by rain and snow only. You can see the spring high water mark on the rocks. Now I'm putting her into fine pitch for landing.'

The engine was louder as the floats touched, skipped, splashed, and they were down in spray. 'That was the best thing ever,' Ian said.

Curtis George turned to stare at him. 'Flying is free life to me,' he said. 'I can see you're going to be another of the same.'

They went ashore at a pebble beach. There were six drums of gasoline on the rocks above. 'I don't know how he got them up there unless the water level was higher in those days. Well, anyway, let's bring four down, two for today and two for tomorrow.'

The drums were heavy, difficult to manoeuvre and restrain. Curtis George sweated, out of breath. 'Never have time for exercise,' he muttered, and sat to rest on a rock.

'Do you have lots of gasoline up there?'

'There were large reserves at the time of the disaster. But they were running low, so for some years our flying has been much restricted. But we have just got our pilot refinery into production.'

'Refinery?'

'The refinery converts crude oil from the earth into gasoline and other useful products. There is more oil in the North than all the old world could have used in fifty years.'

'Oh, I see.'

'Let's get them aboard. I have a winch to do the hoisting.' That part was easy. Ian fixed the cradle round the drum, attached the hook, and the electric winch took it up to be swung into the cabin. Then they loaded the second one, and Curtis George came ashore again. 'It's a slow business,' he said. 'For every drum we bring as far as here, we use nearly four to get it here.' He almost laughed, a sort of snort. He was quite a different man from yesterday, away flying to this other lake where no fish broke the water and no birds moved. It was a bare place between low cliffs, with only a few stunted spruces growing. It was an ugly place.

'Can we go home now? I could still manage half a day at the haying.'

'It's only ten o'clock. We'll have a talk first, and then gas np.'

Ian waited. He felt the change in Curtis George, back to his other self or his real self.

'We knew that there were people at your valley, two houses, we even knew. Who the people were, we did not know. You told me yesterday about your own family, the Smiths. But about the negro family, two families?'

Ian tried to tell him the old story, which had come to him in snatches from his father, his mother, from Mary herself. 'So you see, one of Mary's grandfathers was the botanist, the Parker one, and that was how they came to be here, for a kind of camping holiday in return for making lists of flowers. The other one was the famous one, the student of life, I think it's called a biologist.'

'Yes, a biologist. What was his name?'

'His name was Derwent Morley, Professor Derwent Morley.'

'*Derwent Morley*! But that's amazing.' Curtis George jumped up and walked away, his soft shoes crunching on the pebbles. He stood along there, quite still, his back to Ian. Then he turned to come here again.

'What's amazing?' Ian said. 'I just knew he was supposed to be some kind of a prophet.'

'Some kind of a prophet is exactly what Derwent Morley was. He had made a lifetime study of the algae, plants, mostly tiny, of the oceans and fresh water, and in the early 1970's, some seventy years ago, he achieved by cross-breeding a new strain of algae. Now, most algae are harmless, indeed many useful to man. But the strain that he chanced upon – *chanced upon*, were the words he used – were lethal to all life and to more than life. Morley published a paper on the subject. It was a warning paper, because he saw at once the dangers to the world.

'But the applied scientists of Government knew better. Here, at last, was a way to be rid of the garbage and filth that despoiled the earth. And so, in Morley's absence, they raided his Boston laboratory, and fed the algae while the great tank was being constructed in Florida. It was lined at enormous expense with some special form of leaden glass, immune to the algae, the glass that Morley himself had used to contain them. Then they liberated the algae, and under strictly controlled conditions fed a large proportion of Florida's garbage to them.

'It worked perfectly, but Morley pleaded. He warned and raged and pleaded. *Sooner or later the little monsters will escape*, he said, and he was right. And like other great scientists before him, he felt guilt for what he had brought about. *Starve them to death*, he pleaded, but in vain.

'Ten years remained before a tropical storm burst open the tank, and they escaped. In those ten years Derwent Morley preached. He became a laughing stock but he went on preaching around the world. The more he preached and prophesied, the more he was ridiculed, the more fanatical he became.'

'What's *fanatical*?'

'Fanatical is – let's see – fanatical is your mind burning with ideas so you can think of those ideas and nothing else. Morley preached two things:

'With the first I am in total disagreement. He preached that man's discoveries in science, man's inventions, were so tremendous that they were out of man's control. They had made man their plaything and would destroy him and his world. They were evil.'

'Our fathers both said that. They were hipped about it.'

'It stemmed from Morley, you may be sure. He preached that unless man went back to the horse and buggy, the ox and wagon, the world was doomed. It was a mad philosophy. Man's nature is to seek and go on seeking.

'That was his first belief, a lot of nonsense. But with his second belief I am in entire agreement. In fact Morley's writings have helped me greatly to my own philosophy. He said that the mixing of races, cross-breeding of any kind, have led only to misery and persecution. The whole history of humanity proves this. Furthermore, miscegenation invariably leads to a weakening of stock.'

'So your people don't mate with the black people and the Eskimos?'

'They did,' said Curtis George shortly. 'They do not. I have dealt with that matter, and with the results of it.'

'But look at wee Hamish, he's mixed races, and he's strong, and as happy as he could be, except for a new tooth or something.'

He turned to stare at Ian. It was a blank pitiless stare from those pale eyes. It was perhaps like the stare of the owl bird on the axe. 'Your bastard child is an infant still,' he said, and looked away up the ugly lake.

Ian's neck grew hot, but he must not show anger, he must not. 'Our fathers were hipped about that too.'

'Derwent Morley taught them well,' said Curtis George.

'He didn't teach them. Our grandfathers were all killed before our fathers were old enough to know them. It came down from our grandmothers. They said that for four years every evening before dark, he preached to them at the waterfall. He preached just what you said, and he preached that the Lord took vengeance on us for our sins.'

'What Lord?'

'*The great Lord Alga has struck at last*, he shouted the first time. But then he preached on and on about the Lord being everywhere in everything, and the Lord's displeasure and the Lord's chastisement. The others were terrified. They called him the prophet of the Lord. Mary and I have never understood it.'

'The prophet of the Lord Jehovah,' said Curtis George. He sounded even more thoughtful, darting his tongue and looking at his pudgy hands, palms up. 'I expect that, for their own safety, he was trying to put the fear of God in them. Ian, do you believe in any God?'

'Well, I don't know. I don't think so, but it's difficult.'

'My wife believes all that mumbo-jumbo. I do not. The only god that I believe in is the god that rests in man himself, in me in my cold Arctic home, in you, Ian, in your kindly valley.'

'How do you stand your home if it's so cold up there?'

Curtis George gave a strangled sort of chuckle. 'I meant cold outside. We ourselves live in most adequate comfort in buildings left over from an old defence installation called the Dewline. Here, let me show you a photograph.'

From his pocket he took a leather folder, and a small picture out of that. It was a long low building standing on legs above the snow. 'My headquarters,' he said proudly.

Ian had heard of photographs. 'Do the Eskimos live there too?'

'Oh, no. The Eskimos live in their snowhouses and tents, just as they have lived for thousands of years, and as I fear they always will. I had hopes for the Eskimo, and perhaps if Noel Avakana had lived . . .' His eyes flickered to Ian's face and away. 'If Noel Avakana had lived, he might have done something with his people to fit them for the tasks ahead – in the North only, of course, because they cannot endure heat. But I have had to give that up. They're a hopelessly feckless lot.'

'Feckless?'

'I mean that they live only for today, and never think about tomorrow. They are the hardiest race the world has ever known, but totally without ambition, feckless.'

Now Curtis George handed him another photograph. 'This is my elder daughter, Deborah, taken among the spring flowers of the Arctic.'

It was a coloured picture, not of a cold land at all. The low flowers were pretty and their leaves were green. She was a fair-haired, laughing girl, full-bosomed and lovely. Ian felt a jolt in him. He gave it back. 'She looks happy too,' he said.

'She is,' said Curtis George. He sighed, and a couple of tears rolled down his cheeks. It was most unexpected. 'My Deborah is full of fun,' he said, wiping his cheeks.

He stood. 'Let's gas up now.' He went aboard and handed out two small metal barrels. 'And here are the filter and the pump. It's a slow business. You fill one barrel from the drum up there while I pour the other through the filter. But first we open the drum.'

He used a wrench to unscrew a cap, and then worked the pump handle until the first barrel was full. 'One has to be desperately careful because some water always condenses in the drums. The filter-skin lets only the gasoline through. The smallest amount of water in the tanks means engine failure; that's why I always do it myself. Three tanks,' he said. He sat on one wing, and Ian handed up the barrels to him. Next, he moved to the middle tank above the cabin.

'You were saying yesterday about a big colony of people in the North somewhere else.'

'In Russia,' said Curtis George. He frowned. 'In a part called Siberia. My grandfather's estimate in satellite days was that the two chief settlements comprised about ten thousand and five thousand inhabitants respectively, far larger than any settlement of ours. At the time of Disaster we had oil-men, white and black, among the Arctic islands. We had married families, white and black, at the Thule base in Greenland, and we had one great stroke of luck:

'Of the three SST's that put into Thule when the southern world went dead, two contained women athletes, returning from the Olympic Games. You may or may not know, Ian, that negroid women have exceptional athletic, if not intellectual, gifts. So, many were black women, and a godsend for my grandfather's rather primitive racial policies which my father allowed to lapse (he was a so-called liberal) but which I have brought now to perfection.'

'Those people in Russia, do you talk to them by the radio?'

'In the early days, they were friendly. Not now, though,' said Curtis George Third, waiting patiently for the gasoline to filter before he poured in more. 'They have become increasingly secretive, even downright rude. To our last cordial Christmas message they replied with a question only: *What is Christmas*? My wife was most distressed at that.

'I fear that they plot against us, Ian. I fear that when the great day comes, and the waters of the world are clean again, we shall be forced to take preventive action. Fortunately, they have no intercontinental missiles, nor long-range aircraft. All this we were able to observe in the early days. But in my hands rests what used to be called a first-strike capability.' Curtis George coughed. 'With the utmost reluctance I have reached the conclusion that when the time comes, I must deal with them, or they will swamp us,'

He paused. 'Ian,' he said. 'Even the strongest leader cannot always be an island entire to itself, himself; and I have formed the highest opinion of your potential worth. That is why I am telling you things that I have never even discussed with my senior officers.'

'Well, thanks,' Ian said. 'Did you mean kill all those fifteen thousand Russians?'

'If the worst comes to the worst, in self-defence. I fancy that two single megatons would do the trick.'

'H'mm,' Ian said. 'But when do you think the Lord's pink ocean will be over?'

'Nobody knows, Ian. My scientists were optimistic that it would have been before this. Now they think that the siege may be a long one. It may not even come about in my own lifetime.' He licked his lips. 'All I can do is prepare myself for a great responsibility that may or may not come to me.'

Ian gave him a barrel for the other wing tank. 'Talking of scientific things and the like, you remember that yesterday I said I would send down one of my engineers to teach you. But I have thought further, and it would seem to me that you would learn far more effectively if you were to come North for, say, six months, and study in our machine shops with my leading engineers.'

Shivers went all the way from Ian's neck down his back and to his legs. 'But I couldn't leave home. They could never work the woods and the farm without me.'

'They certainly could if I sent down one good strong man,' said Curtis George Third, and his pink tongue popped again.

'I guess they could,' Ian said. As Mary often said impatiently, he was slow to make up his mind, but he was being forced that way.

Curtis George passed the barrel down to him. 'All full now. Pour the rest back into the drum, screw the cap on tightly and bring down the pump. We can fly at once.' He gave orders in the calm way of a person who knows that he will be obeyed.

He explained again as they circled the lake, roaring the engine, checking switches, he was careful in all that he did. 'No wind,' he said. 'We'll take off South.'

But he did not fly immediately to the South. 'Climb to five thousand feet and then set course.' While they climbed, staying above the safe blue lake, he put what he called the head-set over his ears and fiddled with knobs and spoke into the mouthpiece. He had done the same thing coming up, and he said the same words now, and shook his head. 'Still hopeless,' he said. 'Not a peep out of them. Now on to course.' He spoke in short half-sentences. 'One-seven-eight on the gyro. Going to test fuel tanks.' He put his hand up to a lever switch on the ceiling between them, three positions marked: *port*, *fuselage*, *starboard*. The pointer was in the middle, fuselage, position. He turned the switch left to port, and the engine ran on.

It was obvious that he was testing, not obvious how the switch worked. 'Is it electric?' Ian asked.

'No, manual. Controls are all electronic on the big planes, but this is a simple three-way valve, nothing to go wrong, much better for the workhorse.'

'Is workhorse the name of the plane?'

'No, Muskox, but some workhorse, absolutely stable, flies herself. Plenty of gas again now too, so I'm putting all nine of them back into service.'

Ian listened and watched as they began the journey home. Curtis George switched to the starboard tank and ran on that for a while, then turned to the middle, *fuselage*. 'Flies better with the wing tanks loaded, so I usually run off the fuselage first. Great little plane,' he said, patting the wheel with love.

'You stay on one-seven-eight at five thousand, nose down, nose up, right foot, left foot, bank. That's all you need. I'll do the rest.' He swung the wheel on its long arm over to Ian. 'She's all yours,' he said.

At first Ian did everything too quickly and too much, and the plane swung about and dipped and rose. 'Relax. Lightly, I told you.'

Now it did come easier. Now he loosened his grip. Now soon the Muskox was flying herself, with only a touch here and there from him.

'Good,' said Curtis George, sitting back, arms folded. They flew on South, to the left of the sun at one o'clock. 'Peckish,' he said, whatever that might mean. He got out of his seat, and was back in a minute. He gave a piece of pink fish to Ian. 'Arctic char,' he said. 'Frozen raw. You try it. Warms you up.'

Ian remembered the taste from that other time. It was delicious, crumbling coldly in your mouth like ice-cream. It was chilly up here, but almost immediately he felt the warmth go through him. They flew on South. Flying was easy now, and Ian could think. He had almost made his mind up.

'You're a born pilot,' said Curtis George. 'We'll have you flying in no time flat'.

And you're a natural born wicked bastard, Ian thought, except just perhaps when you're actually flying.

'We can start running off height,' Curtis George said, after much time and much time for thought. 'Nose down a little, airspeed one-thirty. I'm throttling back.'

That was easy too, the altimeter needle unwinding slowly; the needle for the fuselage tank moved slowly back to five gallons or a little more. 'Time to switch,' he said, turning the lever to point to the left to port tank, almost full.

'You can still get a few hours haying in; and then we can fly again tomorrow morning.'

'Sorry,' Ian said. 'I just couldn't. I'd never catch up. I love flying too. I just love it.'

Curtis George did not argue. He could seem to be a very reasonable man. 'Okay, then. The heavy work is done, but I still need a second pair of hands. Well, my wife can come along. All right, Ian, I'll take her now.'

The valley was there below them, a blue and green jewel in dead wilderness. The mower was mowing, that would be Mary. The other three women were pitching yesterday's cured hay into the ox-cart.

'At least five times the population,' said Curtis George Third distinctly, but Ian said nothing. He had made his mind up.

'My wife doesn't much like flying. That's why I let her bring Susan along, keeps her mind off it. On the other hand, the child gets fretful.'

'We could keep Susan tomorrow, if you like. Our mothers would love to have her. They're just crazy about Hamish, and it would be the same with Susan.'

'Thanks. Worth considering.' He turned to head for the waterfall. It had been quite smooth all the way, but there was a horrible bump as they reached the cliff. It bumped Ian's stomach far down and up again. 'Quite a bad thermal,' said Curtis George. 'But nothing to the workhorse.'

They came over the lake, nearly down, now down, home again, safely home.

17

IAN pitched hay all that afternoon. A drying wind came up, but not strong enough to blow wisps of hay around. 'You can pitch more than the rest of us all put together,' said Mary's mother at the barn.

'Such a kindly tireless giant,' said the Reverend Annabel George to Janet Smith. 'You must be proud of him.' She said it quietly, but Ian heard, and was not too happy to hear her say that.

The smell of hay was everywhere, and the children played together in the hay. Then it was time to cook supper, so Ian sent them away, taking over the mower from Mary. When they came back, Curtis George Third had said that he would be working all afternoon on what he called his Master Plan.

'Supper,' Mary called.

He left the mower in the shade of the giant maple at the cabin, unhitched the patient oxen, fed them some grain and turned them out to pasture by the lake.

'The blades on the mower are blunt again,' he said to Mary. 'I'll need to touch them up after supper.' He had killed a calf last evening, so there was tender veal for them and for their visitors.

'Ian, what's happened to your appetite? Are you feeling sick?'

'I feel okay. I guess I just did too much this afternoon.' But perhaps he had thought and worried too much all day to have an appetite. 'How did you get on?'

'We had a lovely time at noon, sitting under the maple tree, the six of us. And I pointed out wildflowers to her, especially the Black-eyed Susans with the same name as Little Susan. She was terribly pleased about that, and she told us some words that Jesus said: *Consider the lilies of the field, how they grow; they toil not, neither do they spin. And yet I say unto you, that even Solomon in all his glory was not arrayed like one of these.*

'And she read us other things from the Holy Bible, which is the Jesus book. Jesus said such decent things.

'So, after we had finished dinner, the old girls took the children for a little toddle by the water's edge, and Annabel and I talked on together, or she talked mostly. She's just mad about that Curtis George. She says he's such a good man underneath, but he lives only for his job as Leader of the Arctic, and preparing himself for when the Lord's pink ocean is all over. And he's the undisputed leader up there, even if the people grumble, but he has a super police force army, absolutely loyal to him. Then she said, and I remember exactly: *But if anything ever happened to Curtis, I'm afraid our northern world would fall apart.*

'And she said that he does seem to be becoming harder, more determined, more alone in himself, and their marriage suffers because of all that, and he doesn't have any energy left to make love to her except occasionally, and that's what she lives for as well as Jesus. And she said that she only had to take one look at me to know that you make love to me all the time.'

'H'mm,' Ian said, half listening.

'It was when we were walking up to start haying after dinner that I managed to be brave enough to ask her again about marrying us. And she stopped and looked down at her toes and shook her head sadly, and she said: *Mary, dear, I can't.*

'So I was a bit angry then, and I said if she could be married to a man who didn't make love to her any more, why couldn't I be married to a man who made love to me morning, noon and night and in-between-times? And wasn't it her job, to marry people? And she said: *Yes, Mary, but I can't, I daren't, because mixed marriages are against State Regulations.* So I said: *Against HIS regulations, you mean?* And she said: *Yes, that's true.* Then she cried a bit. I like Annabel very much, but I hate that Curtis George Third. I hate his guts, even if Jesus said: *Love thine enemies.* So that was all, Ian, except that Annabel said she brought a Holy Bible especially for us.'

'Is that a fact?' he said.

'You're not listening. You're miles away. You're not like yourself at all.'

'Now you listen to me,' he said. 'We're going over to the island to see they're comfortable, and I'm going to say that I have to go round the beasts and then sharpen the mower for tomorrow morning, and I'm going to suggest that they leave Susan at the Grannies' house, and you leave Hamish with them too, and the Georges go with you for an evening stroll up by the wild roses and the woods to the very head of the glen where our wonderful springs gush out, a sight they absolutely mustn't miss. Keep them interested. You could even tell about us and our near-escape that time Outside.'

'But why all this?'

'Never mind,' he said. 'Do what I tell you, and be in your cheeriest mood.'

Ian paddled home. Then he made a quick inspection of poultry, cattle and sheep, all in sleek condition, and to the waterfall and over the bridge to see the beasts on what used to be the Smith side of the lake, and back round by the waterfall again. He paused there a moment. The Lord's pink ocean glowed. It was the colour of the wild rose that bloomed now by the lake, a colour that glowed with life, as the wild rose glowed alive in the sun.

There were threads of pinkness into the backbone of the

river, and pink patches of pond and puddle. But all the land was grey. The buildings of the old town were grey and dead amid that colour and before the sun. The wind had swung from Northwest to South, and on the fitful wind there came of a sudden many scents to touch the nose, some faintly disgusting, some tangy in a prickling way. Ian remembered those smells from other times occasionally. Wind in the South – might that mean fog? But he thought not. The wind of the fog was usually a Southeast wind. There would be no fog unless it changed again. This was the evening breeze from the cold pink sea to the warmer earth. That was the cause, his father used to think. *Like the way the hot smoke rises from the lum and draws in cool air to the fire below.* His dad might have been a lazy man, but he was clever in the old days.

Back at the cabin, Ian watched them cross between hardwoods and evergreens as they climbed towards the head of the valley. He ran along the north shore of the lake where the steep bank hid him. He looked uphill, no one in sight, they would not have reached the high open ground yet. He swam to No-Man's-Island, and followed the path he had taken last night to listen to them talking. Could it only have been last night?

The sun was still high, plenty of time before sunset. *Now, careful!* he told himself, out of sight from everywhere. *Don't hurry.*

It did not take him long. Then he watched in hiding until they had moved from the highest ground down into the woods, and he went home as he had come. He took his stone to the mower blades, which were a little dull, not blunt, but he put a fine edge on them for tomorrow. Inside again, he turned on the electric and sat beside his troublesome steam machine, not to work at it, just to pass the time until Mary came back.

Here she was, with Hamish fast asleep in her arms, and she

carried something else. 'Look, Ian!' she said, 'the Holy Bible that Annabel brought specially for us. See the tiny printing, isn't it lovely?'

Ian looked at it while she tucked Hamish into his cot. He gave the Holy Bible back.

'Did they like it up there?' he asked.

'They thought the gushing springs were super, and they thought the soft green of the valley in the evening sun was perfect. Even that Curtis George was quiet in a different way, and he said: *Some day all our world will be beautiful again. But shall I be spared to see the world I serve?*

'And Annabel spoke without looking at her Holy Bible, just remembering it: *Jesus said to the disciples on a mountain: Take no thought for your life, what ye shall eat, or what ye shall drink, nor yet for your body what ye shall put on. Is not life more than meat, and the body than raiment?*

'*Behold the fowls of the air: for they sow not, neither do they reap, nor gather into barns; yet your heavenly Father feedeth them. Are ye not much better than they?*

'So I said: *If Jesus said that, then Jesus was all wrong. I'm much wickeder than any chickadee or common hen, so how can I be better?*

'And they laughed like anything, even Curtis George Third, but I think he likes Jesus to be stupid. Oh gosh, I'm sleepy after all that haying.'

'Let's go to bed. When are they flying in the morning?'

'As soon as it's light, and they're going to leave Susan with our Mums.'

'That's good.' Ian and Mary went to bed. 'I know what I'm going to do,' she said. 'That bastard won't let her marry us, so I'm going to find the right bit in the Holy Bible, and read it out while I hold your hand, the way that good kind Eskimo made our fathers and mothers hold each other's hands, and then we'll be married, Ian.'

'Okay,' he said. 'Good idea.' But Mary was asleep already.

Ian woke as day was breaking. He lay a while, listening to Mary's quiet breath beside him, and to Hamish breathing lightly, more quickly, across the room. Then he got up and went outside.

There were voices over at the island, his mother and Mary's mother come for Susan. But now there was a whining sound, and chunky-spit, chunky-spit, chunk, chunk to a steady chunking. The flying machine had started up as the rim of the sun came over the hill.

He listened intently to that sound, which ran on evenly, and he went into the cabin. Mary was up, splashing her face with cold water, and Hamish sat on his pot. 'We had such a lovely sleep,' she said. 'Didn't we, Hamish?' He smiled sleepily at his mother.

'We'll have our proper breakfast later. Just milk and an oatcake now. Be quick.'

'What's the hurry, Ian?'

'I want to watch it. Come on!'

He swung Hamish, still eating oatcake and butter, up to sit astride his neck, and he walked fast along the shore path to the waterfall. The flying machine was moving now. It circled the lake once slowly. Then it speeded up, making its own waves and wind, and the wind touched them as it swung away by the waterfall. There was no other wind this morning.

The flying machine roared fast for No-Man's-Island. Was it going up? But the floats had sunk deeper again, and soon the dying roar reached them, and the dying echoes went round the hills.

'Why does it rush around in that stupid way?'

'To warm the engine, and to test the spark,' he said.

'The spark!' She was out of breath from running to keep up

with him and Hamish. 'All this fussing and rushing,' Mary said crossly. 'You're as bad as him.'

'Quiet,' he said. 'We'll watch from here.' He took Hamish down and held him by the shoulders.

'Why not go on to the waterfall?'

'Because I say so. Now it's coming.'

The flying machine was surging before the sound came here. It raced down the lake, faster and faster, lighter and lighter, headed straight for the waterfall. Out of the corner of his eye, Ian saw Mary turn and put her hands up. 'Gosh, Ian!' she cried. 'Gosh, Ian, look! The . . .'

But the roar of the engine drowned what she said. Now the floats were clear, water dripping from them, plucked from them by the wind of speed as the flying machine crossed above the waterfall, headed out over the Lord's pink ocean.

Something was different, wasn't it? He did not notice what was different, for there were spits and bangs. The nose of the flying machine had dropped, more spits and bangs and silence. It went quietly down towards the nearest water, and that was the river, and it was blue, and the river twisted. The flying machine touched the river, safely down on blue water, on *blue* water.

But it was not safely down. It struck a rock at a bend of the river, and flames were spurting before the sound of the crash had reached them here. The flying machine burned up, and a great column of black smoke rose between them and the dead grey town, between them and the clear blue sea.

'Smoke,' Hamish said, a new word of his.

Mary stared at the fire and then at Ian, her young face pinched with horror. 'What happened?' she said. 'What happened, Ian?'

'I did it,' he said, his voice sounding far away outside.

'But poor Annabel! How could you do such a terrible thing?'

'I'll try to explain . . .' Hamish was staring up at him too, an intelligent child. He might remember a word or two and repeat them to his grannies. 'Here, Hamish,' he said, picking fluffy white-tufted grass at a boggy place. 'Wild-cotton, soft tickles on your cheeks.'

As they walked away, there was a flash, and bits of the flying machine flew out from the smoke. The loud explosion came after that.

'But how could you, Ian? What did you do?'

'There were three gasoline tanks on the plane, and a lever-thing you turned to use the left one or the middle one or the right one, and he flew back yesterday on the middle tank until it was nearly empty, then switched to the left one. All I did was turn the pointer back to the middle tank; then I undid the nut that held it and turned the lever so it was pointing to left tank but was really on middle tank. Then I poured a cupful of water each, into the tanks in the wings, he said a tiny amount of water meant certain engine failure.

'That's what I did.'

'But why? How could you do such an awful thing?'

'I'll try to explain,' he said again. He told Mary the things that Curtis George Third had told him, and the things that he had overheard on the island – about the axe, about taking Hamish away to the Arctic orphanage, about wanting Ian to go to the Arctic to learn engineering and sending another man down here – it was not hard to guess what colour of a man he would be – and about what he was going to do to those Russians, and about the base camp in their valley, five times the population. 'It was terrible,' Ian said. 'But what could I do?' He remembered saying that once before, when he had twisted the ladder at the tree house. And he supposed that their fathers had said something like that to one another when they chopped off the heads of those good kind Eskimos. 'I'm just as bad,' he said.

Mary came and put her hands on his shoulders and laid her head across his chest. 'You're not bad,' she said, her lips moving on his chest. 'But why didn't you tell me?'

'Because you can't hide your feelings, and you would have said something angry for sure, and he would have been suspicious. That's why I said: *Be in your cheeriest mood.*'

'That cold wicked beast, he thought he was the smartest man in the world, but you were smarter.'

'I wasn't smarter, I just said nothing. But he was so smart, he couldn't help talking.'

'I think he wanted to talk to you. Coming down the brook last evening he said, sort of to himself: *I see a great future for that young man, trained by me, and linked to me.* "Linked to me," I didn't quite understand, that's like a chain or a family, I guess.'

'H'mm,' Ian said. He saw a girl's picture for a second, but that went away.

'Poor Annabel,' she said. 'You were right, though. Thank the Lord for you.'

Ian turned with Mary in his arms, and he looked over her head at the remains of the flying machine, no flames now, but black smoke rose in a column from it, beside the blue water of the river, against the blue water of the sea. 'The Lord's pink ocean has turned to blue,' he said. 'It really has, but somehow that doesn't seem so strange at all.'

Mary moved away from him and looked there too. 'The earth is all grey, as dead as it could be. How can anything ever grow again?'

'He talked about that. He said that the birds would venture out, and carry seed. And he said that our task was to spread the seeds, little quantities in many places, grass seed and apples and spruce cones and maple seed and everything we could, and gradually the earth would come alive again. That's what he said the day before things happened to the world and him.'

'I suppose you're hotching to go out there, not to spread seeds but to find old guns and bullets and gasoline and machineries from Times Before.'

'I'll wait until I'm sure it's safe,' Ian said, not wanting an argument with his other Mary.

'And then just think of all your lovely new inventions.'

'I'm a man,' Ian said, and he quoted from the late Curtis George Third: 'It's a man's nature to seek and go on seeking.'

'That's just what I mean,' she said, turning her back on him to look along to Hamish, still playing with wild cotton by himself. 'What are we going to say to the next ones when they come?' Mary shivered and caught her breath.

'I've thought of that. They never did get through by radio. So we know nothing about the Eskimos; and these ones came here, but we just saw them crash down when they were leaving to get more gasoline. Actually the plane does a terrific bump at the cliff, so that could have been it. And our Mums don't know what I did. They must never know. Then they'll only have one old lie to change. Do you see?'

'Yes, I see. But what about the bottomless place?'

'I've thought of that too. When the ice gets really thick next winter, I'm going to put hundreds of rocks on the ice above the bottomless place, and nothing can ever float up again.'

'They'll come back. I know they'll come back. One of these days we're going to hear that sound again. I'll be terrified always, listening for it.'

'Some day they will come,' Ian said. 'But Annabel told you, she told you herself that if Curtis George wasn't there to lead them and to drive them, their northern world would fall apart.' He looked at the ocean, calm and clean and blue. 'And when they come down, there will be so much to do, they won't bother us. We used to talk about Times Before, but do you know that already all our pink times are Times Before?'

Mary came to him, and she kissed him with soft passion. 'Oh, Ian,' she said. 'You're strong.'

'Time for breakfast; then time for haying,' Ian said. 'Are you ready for breakfast, wee man?'

But Hamish stared up at him, his dark eyes full of thought. 'Daddy did it,' he said. 'Daddy did it.'

'Yes,' Ian said. 'Daddy did it. Daddy built that bridge along there, where the river goes whoosh, and the waterfall splashes. Daddy did it.'

'Daddy's a snake,' Mary said. 'Daddy's like the grass snake in the grass.'

Hamish, who liked the grass snakes that made Mary shudder, thought that very funny. 'Daddy huge snake,' he said. Ian swung him up, wild-cotton still in hand. 'Tickle Daddy,' Hamish said, and did.

So the small troubled happy family went home. They made hay while the sun shone all that day, and in the evening the white clouds sailed. They cast grey shadows on the sea, and the sun shone on blue sea.

When Hamish and Susan were fast asleep, Mary read to Ian by the light of the Cadillac machine's electric-maker.

'Poor Annabel put in bits of paper to mark a few special good bits. Listen, Ian!

'*To everything there is a season . . . A time to be born, and a time to die . . . A time to kill, and a time to heal . . . A time to weep, and a time to laugh; a time to mourn, and a time to dance . . . A time to love, and a time to hate; a time of war, and a time of peace.*

'She called that part the Old Testament, before Jesus came. *A time to kill* sounds pretty different from what Jesus told them.'

'Yes,' Ian said. He had not forgotten what he had done; and he would not, but it was done.

'This one is Jesus, and I like it best of all:

'*Then there were brought unto him little children, that he should put his hands on them and pray; and the disciples rebuked them.*

'*But Jesus said, Suffer little children, and forbid them not, to come unto me: for of such is the Kingdom of Heaven.*'

The children slept in innocence across the room. Ian put off the light and kissed his fierce tender-hearted Mary, and soon they all were sleeping.

He woke in the darkness of the night to hear a long rumble far away, but Mary did not stir. The sound soon faded. It might have been the rumble of stones and earth sliding down a hill in dead lands beyond. Or it might have been a first stir of those dead lands as life moved again in them. Or it might have been something else.